# Nutcracked

# Nutcracked

## SUSAN ADRIAN

Random House  New York

Text copyright © 2017 by Susan Adrian
Jacket art copyright © 2017 by Stevie Lewis

All rights reserved. Published in the United States by
Random House Children's Books,
a division of Penguin Random House LLC, New York.

Random House and the colophon are registered
trademarks of Penguin Random House LLC.

Visit us on the Web! randomhousekids.com

Educators and librarians, for a variety of teaching tools,
visit us at RHTeachersLibrarians.com

*Library of Congress Cataloging-in-Publication Data*
Names: Adrian, Susan, author.
Title: Nutcracked / Susan Adrian.
Description: First edition. | New York : Random House, [2017] |
Summary: Being cast as Clara in the Nutcracker ballet is a dream come true
for Georgie but when she finds herself sucked into the Nutcracker's world her
dream becomes more real than she ever imagined.
Identifiers: LCCN 2016017172 | ISBN 978-0-399-55668-5 (hardcover) |
ISBN 978-0-399-55670-8 (ebook)
Subjects: | CYAC: Nutcracker (Choreographic work)—Fiction. | Ballet
dancing—Fiction. | Magic—Fiction. | Friendship—Fiction.
Classification: LCC PZ7.A273 Nu 2017 | DDC [Fic]—dc23

Printed in the United States of America
10 9 8 7 6 5 4 3 2 1
First Edition

For my mom,
who got me to all of those classes
and rehearsals and performances for years,
and supported me through everything—

and for Mrs. Crockett, who chose me to be her Clara.
Some of this story is true.

# Prologue

**The Prince surveyed** the people of the Kingdom of Sweets below as he and Clara rose in the bright hot-air balloon. His people waved and cheered. He smiled at the girl beside him, her curls bouncing as she leaned across the edge and waved back. He could not have passed the enchantments or killed the Mouse King without her. But she needed to return home. Clara was young, and this was a long, unexpected adventure. She had not asked to help—she had been brought here by magic. He would follow the Sugar Plum Fairy's instructions and escort the girl safely home, then return, triumphant, to his own kingdom. He stretched out a hand to wave—

There was a shudder so violent that he lost his balance and fell. All went black. It was too sudden to grab hold, useless to struggle. He tumbled over and over, hurtling toward the ground. He expected to hear screams from the crowd, from Clara, but there was only silence. Darkness. Even the rush of air stopped. He did not know how long he had been falling, but he suddenly realized he was lying on something. He had landed without any crash.

He opened his eyes, and his heart sank. Not again. Not after all that struggle, to be returned to the beginning.

The tree towered above him, its top unseeable, miles away. The dark floor stretched into the distance, empty, lit only by the flicker of candlelight. He sat up and hesitantly lifted his hands to his head.

It was too wide, too big, under his hands. Massive teeth grinned against his will.

He heard the distant patter of mice.

The whisper of the old magician returned to his mind. Words he had heard, but not heeded, in his rush to slay the Mouse King and return to his home.

"Let it be so, then. Let this be for two hundred years. . . ."

**N**utcracker audition day is the best, and the worst, day of the year.

It's the best because for one day everything is possible. Being Clara in *The Nutcracker* is right there in the next room, if I can make it happen.

But it's also the worst because I *want* so very badly, hope twisting with the fear of failing in my belly.

I rock back and forth on my toes as the crowd of us wait outside the big studio doors, our numbers pinned to our chests. Half of the others are girls I know, half I don't, all in the same black leotards and pink tights. None of us look at each other, crazy with nerves.

I know I might not get anything this year. I might be too old for the child parts I had before—marshmallow

 3

child, party child, lamb—but not good enough for the real dancer parts that are the next step. I need to prove to Mrs. Cavanaugh that I can do it. That I *am* good enough.

If I am.

I've dreamed of dancing Clara since I was five years old, when Grandpa bought me my green velvet dress and took me to see the show at the Wilson Theater. He folded his big, warm hands over mine as the orchestra started up. During the intermission I leaned over and whispered, "I want to be Clara!"

Grandpa being Grandpa, he raised his eyebrows and said, "Do it, then, Georgie. Make it happen."

But I can't think about Grandpa right now.

I have to think about Clara, the star of the show. She has a solo dance in the first act. She comes onstage by herself at the beginning of the battle scene, her little candle the only light. I'd been so scared, when I was five, that she'd get eaten by the giant mice. But she doesn't. She smashes the Mouse King over the head with her shoe, saves the Prince, and travels with him, through whirling snowflakes, to the Kingdom of Sweets. They ride up in the magic hot-air balloon together at the end, up above all the dancers and the audience, waving goodbye.

I want it all, every one of those moments.

*We* want it all, me and Kaitlyn. Best friends forever. I reach for Kaitlyn's hand and squeeze. It's damp with sweat. She squeezes back, hard.

"Do I look all right?" she asks.

Her number, 14, is a little crooked. My 15 probably is too. We pinned them on each other, since Mom had to go somewhere after she dropped us off. At least Kaitlyn's bun is perfect, a fat, dark coil of hair. I'm good at doing those now. She looks pale, her freckles popping out on her white skin. But otherwise ready to go.

"You look like a Clara," I say.

She flashes me a quick, nervous smile. "You too," she says.

A voice calls from behind the doors, and my heartbeat skips, then pounds louder. Almost time.

Last Saturday after pointe class, the artistic director, Mrs. Cavanaugh, asked both of us if we were planning to audition for Clara. Kaitlyn said that meant she'd chosen us already. I can't let myself believe that, not yet. I might jinx it. But the sliver of hope is there, bright and shiny: Kaitlyn and me, the two Claras, first and second casts. We would be at all the shows together, alternating performances. Our names side by side on the program. It doesn't even matter who gets first cast, as long as it can be the two of us, together. We pinkie-swore yesterday that we wouldn't care.

*If* we get it. *Please, please, please.*

The doors creak open and we all push through, stumbling into the wide-open space of the rehearsal studio. It's beginning. It's really *time.* The room seems too bright, after the semidarkness of the hall. At least it smells familiar: sweat and wood and the sweet sting of rosin, all bundled up together. It's a little bit of comfort.

Mrs. Cavanaugh's daughter Veronica lines us up in rows by number. I stand in my place—near the end of the first line, next to Kaitlyn—and watch Mrs. Cavanaugh. She's standing by the stereo speakers. I wish she'd smile at us or give us a sign, but she doesn't look up. She's in her uniform: she always wears tights, a leotard, and a long, filmy ballet skirt to class and auditions, even though she's old and doesn't dance for real anymore. Her whole outfit today is deep purple, like a queen's.

There are two rows of girls—all the way to number 36. Everyone wants to be Clara. My belly clenches again, a sick twist, and I try to ignore it. It doesn't matter how many dancers are there. She asked us to come. We have a good chance.

One more girl breezes in, number 37, and my stomach drops straight to my toes.

"Ally!" Mrs. Cavanaugh calls, sunny and welcoming.

Kaitlyn and I exchange panicked glances. What is Ally Sinclair doing here? She was second-cast Clara last year . . . and she was *perfect*. Worse, she's always perfect. She's been away in Chicago, at an intensive workshop with the Joffrey Ballet. She couldn't be auditioning for Clara again. Nobody gets to dance Clara twice. Right?

But she's here. Mrs. Cavanaugh leads Ally to the other end of the second row, takes a step back, and nods, gnarled hand on her chin, her ring flashing. "You've hardly grown at all," she says. Her smile falls off and she scans the rest of us, eyes sharp. I think they rest on me and Kaitlyn. I stay perfectly still, just in case. She claps her hands. "Let's get started."

She shows us the doll dance, which is ridiculously easy. A lot of us did it last year as party girls, lined up in our colorful dresses behind Clara. Step, step, hop, turn, rock a pretend doll. She has us dance it to the music in groups of ten.

I forget to feel jittery while I'm dancing *that* . . . until I watch Ally, in the last group. She moves so smoothly from one step to the next, her feet pointed exactly right, smiling. Her arms are always curved perfectly, her fingers graceful but natural. I wonder if I did it that well.

I don't know if I could have. She'll probably get Clara. There's no reason not to give her the part. And then what happens to us? I look at Kaitlyn while we're waiting for everyone else to be done. She's frowning, staring at the other girls, her freckles so clear it's like they were drawn on with marker.

When the last group finishes the doll dance, Mrs. Cavanaugh thanks us and asks us to wait while she speaks with Veronica. They mutter and whisper and mark things on their paper while my body stays still but my pulse does jetés on its own. When she steps forward, the room goes quiet, all the air sucked out of it at once. She takes a breath, looks at us over her narrow glasses, then reads off the cuts.

I'm not cut. Kaitlyn isn't either. But a lot of girls are, way more than half. All the non-studio girls—Mrs. Cavanaugh wouldn't choose an outside girl for Clara—and the ones who aren't quite good enough yet. I do a quick count of how many are left: twelve. Kaitlyn and I tap our thumbs together in a mini high five that no one else can see.

But we're not there yet.

Mrs. Cavanaugh turns to face the mirrors again and shows us Clara's solo dance, the one she does in the party scene to celebrate getting the Nutcracker. I know that one too. The party girls practiced the Clara dance last year while the other cast rehearsed—in case both Claras got sick, or kidnapped, or enchanted by an evil fairy, and one of us had to suddenly take the part and save the show.

It could've happened.

This dance isn't very hard either. Step, step, hop, with some chassés and a single pirouette and a few other small step and runs, carrying a pretend Nutcracker to show him off. We hold our hands up high, empty, and show off to the mirrors.

We dance it in three groups, and when we're done, we have to stand and wait again. I itch to do something to keep warm and melt my twitching nerves—elevés or tendus or anything—but Mrs. Cavanaugh's eyes fall on me and I stay still, hands folded the way she likes when we're not dancing. Professional.

She studies me for a full two seconds while I don't breathe at all, then turns back to Veronica. They talk and we wait. And wait.

The dream is so close to coming true, and so close to ending, at the same time.

Mrs. Cavanaugh claps her hands and steps forward, and I squeeze my fists hard, my nails digging into my palms. I want to close my eyes too, to make the moment stay in case it's the last one before I find out it's a no. But I can't. I have to just stand there and let it happen.

"Numbers 14, 15, and . . . 37," she says, her voice smoke-scratchy.

Me and Kaitlyn!

And Ally.

"Please stay. The rest, thank you so much for coming. That will be all."

Me, Kaitlyn, and Ally, the *last three*. I want to scream loud enough to rattle the mirrors. I bounce on my heels and quick-look at Kaitlyn, our eyes meeting in a burst of hope. But we keep our faces blank while we wait for the others to file out. I feel bad for the girls I know. It's awful to be cut at the end.

But I'm still here. *We* are still here. For now.

2

**A**fter everyone is gone, Mrs. Cavanaugh crosses her arms and stands in front of us, her feet turned out. She lifts her chin. "Thank you, girls. You have all done well. We are having a difficult time deciding among the three of you."

I make my back as straight as I can, pull in my hips. Keep my eyes on her face. It feels like my eyes are bigger than usual, the muscles around my mouth tighter. It's a good sign if they're not absolutely sure they want Ally. It could still be me and Kaitlyn.

Or it could be Ally and Kaitlyn. I flinch.

"We'd like you to do the Nutcracker dance again," Mrs. Cavanaugh says. "Veronica?"

Veronica doesn't really look like Mrs. Cavanaugh—

she has long black hair she wears in a swinging pony-tail, and there aren't any lines in her face. Her eyes are the same, though. She steps forward, holding a wooden box the shape of a shoe box but bigger, scuffed and worn. Words in a language I don't know are burnt into the lid in a dark swirl of letters. The box looks as if it's been in a dusty attic. Or a magic wardrobe. Or in the hold of a ship, carried across the ocean.

I want to touch it and run my finger across the writing.

"This is a very special Nutcracker." Mrs. Cavanaugh rests her hand gently on the edge of the box. She looks at each of us in turn, like she's trying to tell us something. Ally nods, cool. Of course. She did this last year. She glances at me, and I swear she sniffs.

"He's been handed down in my family for genera-tions," Mrs. Cavanaugh continues. "I want you to do the dance with him like you're onstage. You just got him as a gift from your beloved, slightly mad uncle Drosselmeyer for Christmas, and you're thrilled. You know he's a magi-cian, so the Nutcracker must be wonderful. Magical." She studies us again. "Kaitlyn, you go first."

She's not using the numbers anymore. Probably since

it's only the three of us, and she knows us. I like that. Though she knows Ally best.

Veronica opens the box and holds it out as if it's precious, like my dad with his championship football. I get a good look at it.

I shiver.

The Nutcracker has a huge head, with stringy black hair that's starting to rub off. It looks like real hair. His—Its? No, his—teeth make me think of the wolf's in the Red Riding Hood story, yellow and massive, his lips pulled back to show them off. The Nutcracker has a Russian-soldier outfit painted on, and a strange little crown. I can smell him from here, musty wood, and an under-smell I can't figure out. His black eyes look like they're watching me.

I've seen him before, of course, in rehearsals and onstage when Clara was holding him. But I've never really looked at him as anything except another prop.

Kaitlyn steps forward, awkward, her nose scrunched up. She hesitates, then quickly shoves her hands into the box and pulls the Nutcracker into her arms. I can tell she'd rather be doing anything than touching him—she doesn't like old things or dirty things—and I hope Mrs. Cavanaugh doesn't notice. It feels important how we treat him. Ally and I slide out of the way, back against the barres, and Kaitlyn goes to the starting position.

The music begins, and she takes the first steps.

She trips on the first pirouette.

Kaitlyn freezes, her cheeks blooming pink, and Mrs. Cavanaugh gestures to stop the music. "Start again," she says kindly. "From the beginning."

It's quiet while Kaitlyn walks back to her place, the Nutcracker pinned under her arm. She gets in position again, then glances at me. I show her two thumbs up before her eyes drop, and the music goes.

This time she gets the steps, but something's wrong. Every move looks wooden, stiff. Even her smile seems like it might crack or wither away. It's not real, any of it, and you can tell. Five-year-old me would have been able to tell it wasn't right, that she wasn't enjoying the dance. Or *getting* it, feeling what it would be like to be Clara.

I wonder if she's just too nervous. She's not going to get Clara dancing that way. Unless I do worse, somehow.

I feel sick. I want Kaitlyn to do well. *And* me to do well. Not this.

Mrs. Cavanaugh lets her dance all the way through. There's a horrible pause when the music ends, and Kaitlyn thrusts out the Nutcracker like she's desperate for someone to take him from her.

"Georgie," Mrs. Cavanaugh says, expressionless.

I have to do my best. I can't mess up like Kaitlyn did. I've wanted this for so long.

I lift the Nutcracker from Kaitlyn, careful, and she scurries off to the side with Ally. He's heavy, rigid. I hold him up over my head and smile, a stage smile, but really pleased too. I carry him to the corner cradled in my arms the way Clara does after Drosselmeyer gives him to her in the show. I swear the Nutcracker is watching me. The smell is stronger now, with something spicy underneath, like cinnamon sticks and cloves. It's nice up close. I like it. He even feels a tiny bit warm.

I hardly see the audition room anymore. Holding the Nutcracker in my arms, I rock him a little, pretend I'm a girl in the 1800s who has just gotten an amazing present.

The music starts, and I dance.

It's the same dance we just did, so I don't have to think about the steps. And I don't, at all. I don't think about the audition or my nerves or the pressure. I don't think about Kaitlyn or what will happen if I don't get the part. Instead, I focus on the Nutcracker I'm holding. I focus on smiling, doing the steps. And most of all, being Clara.

I don't notice at first that everything seems bigger. Chairs loom over me, with strong wooden legs the size of telephone poles. There are presents as big as I am, wrapped in shiny foil paper, with curls of satin ribbon I could wrap around myself for a dress. The floor is dark wood, miles of it, polished so smooth I can see the reflections of the candles way up high. And a Christmas tree . . . I sense more than see it behind me, a great forest of branches I could climb for weeks and never reach the top. I smell it too, the rich holiday scent of pine, a touch of hot wax. It's dark, and I'm alone, dancing with my Nutcracker. . . .

A tree? Presents? This isn't the studio.

I stop just as the music does. The floor, the tree—all of it vanishes. I stand there, blinking, clutching the Nutcracker, looking at my own wild face in the mirror.

"Well done, Georgie." Mrs. Cavanaugh smiles, small but like she means it, her voice rich with praise. "Ally, you next."

17

I hand the Nutcracker to Ally as if I'm in a dream, and I drift over to Kaitlyn. I did well? I don't even remember dancing, not after the first bit. All I remember is that room: huge, grand, echoing, and empty. What was that?

I reach for Kaitlyn's hand, but her fingers slip out of mine. She doesn't look at me, her eyebrows drawn together tightly as she stares at Ally. I want to say something, but I can't talk now, in the middle of the audition.

She couldn't be mad at me for doing well, could she?

Ally smiles over her shoulder at us, then dances perfectly. Of course. She hands the Nutcracker to Veronica when she's done. Veronica takes him reverently, tucks him into the box, and closes the lid.

The air lightens somehow, and my head feels clearer. I look at Kaitlyn again, but she still keeps her eyes turned away, her jaw clenched.

I step away from the barre and take my waiting stance, and so does Ally. Then Kaitlyn. We wait, the three of us in a row, all staring hard at the mirror while Mrs. Cavanaugh and Veronica decide our fates.

This is the divide: on one side Clara and triumph and dreams, on the other side nothing. Failing.

It doesn't take as long this time.

"Kaitlyn." Mrs. Cavanaugh's black eyes are glass beads, glittering. "I'm very sorry, but not this year. Ally, you will be our first-cast Clara. Georgie, you will be second cast." She takes a step toward us and sets one hand on Ally's shoulder, the other on mine, as light as a butterfly. "Congratulations, girls."

Kaitlyn takes a hiccupy sob of a breath and hurries out of the room.

I stare up at Mrs. Cavanaugh, at Ally next to me smiling widely, and for a second I really, honestly can't breathe. I put a hand to my chest like I need to push to remind myself how. The breath comes, but the wonder doesn't stop.

I did it, for real. I'm going to be Clara. Onstage with the balloon and the Nutcracker and *everything*.

I did it. But Kaitlyn didn't.

**3**

**A**lly shoots out of the studio and leaps at her mom, right there waiting by the door. "I got it! First cast!"

Her mom squeals and squeezes her in a bear hug. They don't notice Lissa leaning against the wall alone, tears flooding down her cheeks. She was cut in the second round. I know Lissa pretty well, even if we're not *friends*.

I catch her eye and frown in sympathy.

She sniffs and glares at me with her red eyes, and I decide to keep walking past. I need to see Kaitlyn first. Then my mom. She said she'd be here too, waiting.

A flock of little boys are lined up on the other side of the hall, ready to go in, rattling off the walls with excitement. I think they're trying out for Fritz, my onstage little

brother, so I should probably pay attention to who's in line, but I don't.

Clara. I skip a few steps, because I can't help it. I can't wait to tell Mom. I don't care if it's second cast. I got *Clara*. For real. I'll get to do eight performances, same as Ally.

But then I think of Kaitlyn. How can I be happy when it isn't both of us being Clara, together? I don't know what I'm going to say when I see Kaitlyn. *I'm sorry*? But it feels empty. How do you say you're sorry for winning something you've always wanted?

I decide for right now to focus on getting the part, not on Kaitlyn's *not* getting it, at least until I tell Mom. I want to hold on to the happiness part first.

A whisper flies ahead of me down the hallway—*Ally and Georgie, it's Ally and Georgie*—and people start to congratulate me, girls from my class, some of the boys trying out for Fritz, and older dancers I didn't even think knew who I was. I beam at everyone and walk faster. It's as if I've won a contest or the lottery, and everyone wants to know me all of a sudden. Everything's shiny.

*Shiny.* I stop, an image of that shiny foil paper, the massive tree, flashing in my mind. Was any of that real, or was it some strange, vivid thing I imagined? I've never seen anything like it before. The world was gone, and all I saw was that other place.

I keep pushing down the long hallway, past company girls breaking in pointe shoes, then into the lobby past moms measuring kids and pinning numbers. I see Mom through the glass doors, standing in the parking lot. The sun shines bright on her white shirt. Pippa's clinging to her leg, and she's bouncing Will, who's screaming his head off, his face purplish. Now that I see them, I can even hear him through the doors and all the chatter in the lobby.

Suddenly I can't wait another second to tell her. She'll be so proud of me.

I bolt for the door, yank it open, and throw myself at her like Will isn't even there, like I'm not wearing my ballet slippers on the pavement. "I got it! I got Clara!"

"Oh, baby, that's wonderful!" Her voice is muffled by my hair. Will, squished between us, screams harder. Mom pulls away gently and strokes my cheek with her thumb. "I'm so proud of you!"

She *is*. I feel it, as though I'm curled up in a warm comforter. She's not like a lot of the other moms, who are at the studio all the time. She doesn't do my hair or sew ribbons on my shoes. But she smiles, and I can tell she's proud. Her eyes are brown with little gold sparks in them, just for me. I beam and hug her again.

"Sorry I was late," Mom says. "I was on the phone with Grandma."

A chill flicks through me. "Is Grandpa okay? Is there news?" Grandpa Reynolds—Dad's dad, my favorite—had a stroke two weeks ago and hasn't woken up since. He's in the hospital, no kids allowed. Grandma says he's going to be just fine, wait and see, but it feels like a big rock in my chest whenever I think about it.

"No change," Mom says.

I swallow, the sound loud in my ears. I ache to tell Grandpa that I got the part. He's the one who told me to go for it. He's come to every *Nutcracker* performance I've been in, sometimes sixteen times in one year.

I bury my face in Mom's shoulder for a second. She rubs my back. "It'll be okay," she murmurs.

The door opens behind us. "Georgie?" says Julia, the

dance school administrator. "Congratulations, dear. I need you to come in and get your rehearsal schedule. Mom, I need the paperwork signed and a casting fee."

Mom's wrinkles show around her eyes, and she bounces Will again. "Casting fee?"

"Two hundred dollars, yes, to cover costumes and production costs. For the major parts." Julia winks at me and glides back inside gracefully.

Mom sighs. She swings Will back and forth, and he finally starts to settle down. "Get your sister, please, Georgie." Over Mom's shoulder I see my sister Joey sitting on the curb, her chin resting on her fists. She looks bored, like Mom dragged her here. I take Pippa's hand, pretending that's what Mom meant, but Mom jerks her chin toward Joey. Then she heads for the door with Will.

She stops, one hand on the door, and looks back over her shoulder. "What about Kaitlyn?"

I shake my head. "Ally Sinclair."

"Oh." Mom nods, understanding instantly. "We'll talk when we finish this, okay?" She smiles, her eyes crinkling up, then disappears inside.

"Come on, Jo. We have to go in," I try from where I am. Joey doesn't move. I was pretty sure she wouldn't.

I tug Pippa—she's four, and tuggable—over to where Joey's sitting. "You heard Mom. We have to go inside."

Joey stands with a loud, dramatic sigh. She's nine. She smells like potato chips. *"Fine."*

"Come on," I say, and lead the way into the studio.

Julia hands me my rehearsal schedule, printed out on sheets of green paper with the *Cavanaugh's Dance Company* logo at the top. I'm surprised to see I'm not just Clara. I've been given a role as a soldier for the other cast too, in the first-act battle scene. With two roles, there are a *lot* of rehearsals. Evenings on Monday, Wednesday, and Thursday, and most of Saturday for the rest of September and all of October. Then in November we start going every day until performances begin in early December. Seven days a week, with full rehearsal days on weekends.

I feel fizzy, happiness bubbling up inside me. It's real. I'm really going to do this.

I'm going to do nothing but this until December.

Mom hands Julia a check for the casting fee. I wonder

how my parents are going to be able to get me to all these rehearsals. Dad's got football practices and games, plus there's school for all of us and Joey's karate lessons, and whatever else comes up. If Kaitlyn had gotten it too, we would've been able to carpool.

I look at my schedule again and whisper to myself, *"Clara rehearsals."* For real.

I hand the schedule to Mom and clutch Pippa's hand so hard she squeals and yanks it out of my grasp. I swoop up both her hands again and spin her around like an airplane, right there in the lobby, until she laughs and laughs. For this moment I don't care who's in the way or who's watching. I can forget everything else. I'll go find Kaitlyn in a minute, but for right now I have to celebrate.

And then Kaitlyn's mom comes through the doors. She sees me swinging Pippa, sees Mom bouncing Will and signing things, and the frown on her face deepens. I let Pippa's hands go.

"Joanna," Mom says. "I'm sorry—"

Kaitlyn's mom waves a hand. "Don't bother. I'll take Kaitlyn home." She lowers her head and disappears up the stairs, to the dressing rooms.

I should have looked there before celebrating. I should have gone up to make sure she was okay. I left her alone after she got rejected from the role she wanted most. What kind of best friend does that?

I turn to Mom, not sure what I should do. If Kaitlyn's mom is angry, what did Kaitlyn tell her?

"I'm sure she's upset," Mom says softly. "Maybe it's best if you just see her Monday."

Maybe. I don't think Kaitlyn would really be mad at *me*—it's not my fault. But it might be awkward, especially because I didn't go find her. So I don't change yet. I wait until she comes down with her mom, her face red and puffy, walking carefully on the far side of the room, and I let her leave without saying anything.

It feels absolutely wrong. I can't sit and wait until Monday. I'll call her tonight or tomorrow, and we'll talk and everything will be smooth again. And then Monday I can tell her about how exciting all of this is.

I wanted it to be Kaitlyn and me, more than anything. But I hope there's a way we can both be happy even though it's just me.

# 4

**W**hen I get to school on Monday, I don't know what to do.

Kaitlyn didn't answer my call on Saturday night. On Sunday her mom answered, but she said Kaitlyn wasn't home in a way that made me not believe her at all. Afterward I stared at the phone like I could make it ring, make her call me back, but nothing happened.

I never go this long without talking to Kaitlyn, especially when there's something important to talk about. We've been best friends since the middle of first grade, when my family moved here because Dad got his job at the high school. I signed up for Mrs. Cavanaugh's, and Kaitlyn was there too. We've been together ever since, in the same dance classes, together at school, working our way up.

Working our way up to being Clara.

Ever since that first class, we've done all ballet things together. We're about the same technique-wise, and we're the same height, so the teachers often pair us up. It's always been Kaitlyn and Georgie, Georgie and Kaitlyn, everywhere.

When we were Mother Marshmallow's children together, our first year in *The Nutcracker,* we used to watch the first act from our spots on the floor, side by side. Mostly we just giggled our way through, but we were always quiet for Clara's dances. The next two years, as party children, we'd practice Clara's dances. It seemed like the biggest deal to be Clara. One day you were just another girl in the school, and the next you were the one everyone was watching.

I feel like I'm divided in pieces, like the pie charts you do in math. Half is happy I'm really Clara, the running-down-the-street-shouting-it kind of happy. A quarter is sorry for Kaitlyn. And a quarter—no, less than a quarter . . . an eighth? I'd label it in tiny letters so no one would see, it's so wrong, but an eighth is mad at Kaitlyn for being mad at me.

So I stand outside the cafeteria, where we always meet, for five minutes longer than usual, but no more than that. Because she should come, and I don't understand why she doesn't. But she clearly *isn't* coming. Then I bite my lip, hitch up my backpack, and head to first period.

We're in different homerooms this year, so we don't have any of the same morning classes. That's why we meet early, to walk to class together and talk everything over before we start. *Everything,* from school to ballet to our crazy families.

It feels lonely starting the day without her.

But I'm Clara. I want to keep hugging that to myself, even if no one else knows yet, even if not many people would care if they *did* know. I let a thrill of excitement run through me. My first Clara rehearsal is tonight!

I sit at my desk in homeroom, and Sierra, next to me, asks why I'm smiling. I shrug and get out my book. I'm not ready to share the Clara news, not yet. With Kaitlyn upset, it would feel like bragging. But I write *Clara* really small on the edge of my notebook paper so I can look at it anytime I want.

· · ·

**At lunch I head** for our table, but Kaitlyn's not there. Our spots, on the end across from each other, are empty. I scan the cafeteria. Nothing. Maybe she didn't come to school today. Maybe she's sick. I should call her again tonight and make sure she's all right.

Mio, one of the girls in Advanced Track with me, calls me over, so I sit with her and a group of other AT girls. I eat my PB&J and let their talk about TV and movies and the new boy in P.E. wash over me without ever diving in. It's still lonely, but somehow I make it through lunch without Kaitlyn.

After lunch is my favorite period: reading. I still can't believe it's an actual class. The people who need help with reading work with the teacher, Mr. Anderson. But those of us who don't need help get to use the time to read whatever we want (as long as he approves it) and write a report afterward. Whatever we want! I'm reading *A Wrinkle in Time*. I love it. It's magic and adventure and it's wonderful, and I wish it would happen to me.

Anyway, a full forty-five minutes a day when I'm not just *allowed* to read but *expected* to is the best. And Kaitlyn's in the class too, so we usually hang out in the back corner and read side by side. The only challenge is not talking.

At least, that's usually the challenge. Today I step into class expecting to sit alone.

But Kaitlyn *is* here. She's back in our corner, her book open on the desk, her whole body hunched. She looks uncomfortable.

I hurry over and drop my bag next to my chair. "Hey. Are you okay? I was worried when I didn't see you at lunch."

She doesn't answer, doesn't even look up. I stand there awkwardly. Maybe . . . she didn't hear me?

"Kaitlyn," I say.

Her head snaps up like a puppet's, and I take a step back when I see her face. Her expression is hard and sad. Her eyes, normally bright blue, look cloudy. Her voice scrapes out like it would rather not. "I don't want to talk to you, Georgie."

I frown. "I don't under—"

"I don't want to talk to you! Leave me alone!" This time it's louder, and Mr. Anderson clears his throat up at the front of the room, even though the bell hasn't rung yet.

The pie-chart Georgie is one-quarter mad now. But one-quarter is still sorry for Kaitlyn. So I don't respond. I just stand there. Then I pick up my backpack and move to the other side of the room, to an empty seat next to a boy I've also known since first grade, Noah Waterston. He raises his chin at me—he heard, everyone did—and I drop into the seat, dig out my book, and try to shut out the world and read. But my eyes are wet, and it's hard to see.

Thinking of Clara doesn't even make me feel better. All I can see is Kaitlyn's sad face.

I don't know how to fix this. But there has to be a way. She can't keep being mad over something that's not my fault.

Can she?

**5**

**The first rehearsal.** The real start of being Clara.

Tonight it's only me, Ally, the two Fritzes, and Mrs. Cavanaugh in the big rehearsal room—which is the biggest classroom, the same one we had auditions in. It's so strange having a group this small in the big space. It's as though we're real dancers, important and serious.

Well, it would be if my Fritz, Justin, would stop leaping around like a rubber ball. He's seven, and he's in Veronica's class for boys. He does look a little like me, fair and blond and smallish. Maybe what my brother, Will, might look like when he's older. Ally's Fritz, Caleb, has dark hair like Ally's.

Justin jumps around the room with both feet together, pretending he's a kangaroo. Caleb sits on the floor next to Ally, perfectly behaved, as he's supposed to.

Mrs. Cavanaugh talks to us about the responsibility we have, that she's trusting us with the most significant roles in the show and that we have to promise to work very hard for her. When she rests her dark eyes on me, I try to be taller, stronger. I want to do every step perfectly. She takes us to a monitor in the corner to show us a video of last year's *Nutcracker,* the party scene. There's always a video of the first cast for the archives, taken during the final dress rehearsal. I recognize Julianne, last year's first-cast Clara. She's in the junior company now. Last year Ally was in second cast, but she'll be Clara in the video this year. I'll be a soldier in the video.

I don't mind. Being second cast doesn't matter. I still get to be onstage alone with the candle, run away from the mice, and go up in the balloon.

On-screen, Drosselmeyer gives Clara the Nutcracker at the party. She hugs him, then runs back and does the dance, the same one we did in the audition. But here her little brother, Fritz, is harassing her the whole time, reaching for the Nutcracker . . . until he finally steals it and stomps it in half. He pretends to onstage, anyway. Justin hops from foot to foot next to me, not even paying attention. Hop.

Hop. Hop. Like a crazed rabbit. He has to stop or he'll get in trouble. He can't start off this way.

"Justin!" I whisper. "Watch the video, okay?"

Mrs. Cavanaugh frowns at *me*.

Oops.

After that I let him hop, and watch the screen instead. I see myself last year, in my orange-and-pink party dress as a first-cast party child, shaking my finger at Fritz like I'm supposed to.

The video zooms in as Clara holds the Nutcracker high, and I see him again, the odd little Nutcracker we danced with at the audition.

"Where does the Nutcracker come from?" I blurt out.

Mrs. Cavanaugh sighs, presses Pause, and looks at me, her thin eyebrows curved high. Everyone looks at me. Even Justin stops the hopping.

"Yes, Georgie?" Mrs. Cavanaugh says, fake-polite. "What was it you absolutely needed to interrupt our rehearsal time with?"

I swallow, wishing I could reel the words back into my mouth. "I was wondering about the Nutcracker."

The screen is paused on a close-up of his face, the eyes

wide and yellow teeth bared. He's ugly if you only glance at him. But there's something underneath, something about him that makes me want to smile.

Mrs. Cavanaugh tilts her head, bits of gray hair escaping from her long braid in puffs around her face. She looks like a bird, gray feathers all rumpled. "Ah." Her voice warms. "Yes. As I said at the audition, he is a family heirloom from Prussia. He is very, very old. When I spoke of the trust I'm giving you? That is part of it. You will only dance with him onstage and in this room, and I trust each of you will treat him with the utmost care and respect, always. He means a great deal to me. Is that clear?"

We nod solemnly, even Justin.

"Now that you understand the procedures—" She pauses. "Is that all?"

"Yes." I say it softly, just loud enough for her to hear, and she presses Play.

We silently watch the dance to the end, then one more time with Mrs. Cavanaugh pointing out the blocking, where everyone is supposed to be onstage for the different parts.

Ally and Caleb go first. Justin and I sit on the floor, our backs against the cool mirror, and watch. Mrs. Cavanaugh acts the part of Drosselmeyer, handing Ally the Nutcracker with a grand flourish. She's good. I can almost see crazy Drosselmeyer looming there, in a suit and an eye patch and flowing white hair. She said once that the magic of dancing is making people see what isn't really there.

Ally only gets a few steps into the solo dance when Mrs. Cavanaugh stops her for not holding the Nutcracker high enough. She tells Caleb he wasn't in the right place. They go back and start again. This time they get further, but it's unpredictable when Mrs. Cavanaugh will stop, for arms or timing or feet. The Fritzes don't have much actual dancing in this part, mostly chasing Clara with stage running and a little bit of kicking, but still Caleb has to be in the right place at the right time. They practice seven times before they make it all the way to the end, with Caleb fake-stomping the Nutcracker. Mrs. Cavanaugh waves her hand.

"All right, let's try Georgie and Justin now."

I feel a little sick as I push to my feet—almost worse than the audition. I want to please Mrs. Cavanaugh and justify her choosing me over everyone else. Especially over Kaitlyn.

I take my place at the starting mark.

"Relax," Mrs. Cavanaugh says, her voice almost rough. "I'm not going to slap you if you mess up."

I try a smile, not looking at Ally, and shake it off. I know this dance. It'll be fine.

The music swirls, and I run forward to Mrs. Cavanaugh-as-Drosselmeyer to collect my Nutcracker.

The moment I take him in my hands, my head gets foggy, as if there's a layer of cloud between me and everything else. The Nutcracker feels almost warm, like before. I run back to my place anyway, focusing on him in my arms, his teeth forever smiling. I rock back and forth, twice, then start the dance.

I'm in the room again, the same strange room I saw at the audition. It's still giant, with the shining floor, the massive chairs, and the forest of a tree. The smell of pine and candles fills the air.

I thought I'd imagined it. But maybe not?

I'm not dancing this time. Now I'm standing in the middle of the floor, alone, in a heavy, cream-colored, old-fashioned nightgown and soft ballet slippers, like Clara's costume in the show. No, not alone. Across the room, by the Christmas tree, is a tall, misshapen shadow. . . .

"Georgie! I said stop, please."

I stop, though I didn't know I was dancing, and stare around me, disoriented. What just happened? How was I there—wherever *there* is—and here at the same time? Why don't I remember the dancing?

"You did fine, Georgie. No notes on that part. Justin, though . . ."

She gives him corrections while I stand there, lost, holding the Nutcracker. I wonder if that's going to happen again. Mostly I think of that shadow, waiting for me. It was man-size. But it definitely wasn't a man.

When it's time to go back to the beginning, my hands are shaking. The music starts, with the familiar violins, and I take a step.

I'm there again. The shadow is still there, not moving. The shape of a tall man, but with a giant square head.

He steps forward into the flicker of the candlelight, and I gasp. It can't be! It's a full-size version of the Nut-cracker, *my* Nutcracker. But this isn't part of a costume, like the one we use onstage. This head is real. Horrible. The music of my dance still plays, distant.

"Do not be afraid, please."

His voice is low and round, resonating in my chest. Strangely soothing. I want to trust it. I want to reach out to him and touch his strange head, but I don't dare. The eyes study me, the same eyes as the Nutcracker doll's.

"Clara, I must ask for your help."

The music stops. I blink, and I'm in the studio again. Mrs. Cavanaugh is eyeing me strangely—so is Ally, from the floor—but she gives a tiny shrug. "Well done, Georgie. Justin, what *are* you doing with your arms? That is not what I showed you at all."

I stand, waiting, not looking at the Nutcracker in my hands, at his eyes on me. We're not done with the dance yet, so we're going to start from the beginning again. And now I know what will happen when we do. I'll go back to wherever that is, and Mrs. Cavanaugh and the others won't even know I'm gone. My body will be dancing like it's supposed to, but *I* will be somewhere else.

I'm scared, honestly. I don't understand what's happening at all.

"Places," Mrs. Cavanaugh says, and I head slowly back

to the corner, dazed. I have to dance. I can't tell her that I'm going to another world, to some big old-fashioned room, or I'll sound completely crazy.

The music starts again, and I tense, but I take the first steps.

It's as though I never left. We stand in the same spots, in the big room, and I'm facing the Nutcracker.

"Please," he says, speaking quickly now. It's odd, because his mouth doesn't move at all. "I cannot defeat him on my own. I need a Clara to help me. *I need you.* It is different this year. It has been two hundred years since it started, and that's when he said it would end. I fear this is my last chance to return to my home. Will you help?"

I look around at this beautiful, towering room, the strange Nutcracker-man looming over me. It's perfectly still, like everything is holding its breath, waiting.

He steps closer and whispers, almost in a singsong:

> *"One battle ended,*
> *Two links forged,*
> *Those who are lost shall be found."*

I swallow. I don't know what that means. I don't know what any of this is—at all—but either it's a strange hallucination or it's magic in some way. It doesn't feel like a hallucination. It *feels* like magic. The Nutcracker has felt magical from the very beginning.

I believe in magic. I read about it all the time. And Grandpa tells me stories about it, stories that feel real, about objects and places that hold power. In the stories, magic requires a choice. If I say no, this probably won't happen again, coming here. If I say yes . . .

The music stops, and I'm back in the rehearsal studio. "Very nice, Georgie. Yes," Mrs. Cavanaugh says. "Justin, you're getting closer. Okay, Ally and Caleb, let's try you again."

Ally stands, and I have to hand the Nutcracker back to Mrs. Cavanaugh. I feel suddenly cold without him.

We sit on the floor, and I stare toward Ally and Caleb, but I don't really see them. Or Justin, tapping his feet next to me.

Is it real? I think it is. It's happened four times now. You don't have the same hallucination four times, right? The place and the Nutcracker feel real; they just feel . . . different. A different sort of place, or time, from this one. I think of the books I read. *A Wrinkle in Time. The Dark Is Rising. 100 Cupboards.* There's always a magical world where it's dangerous, but necessary, to go.

The Nutcracker said he needed my help. He said I was the *only* one who could help.

I want it to be real. But if I accept that it is, I have to decide. Without knowing what I'd have to do, should I say I'll help him?

"Yes," I whisper, though no one could possibly hear me.

"Georgie and Justin, one last time tonight," Mrs. Cavanaugh says. "Come on, places."

Now that I know my answer, I rush to my place. I'll tell him yes. I wonder if it'll happen tonight, whatever I have to help him with.

I take the Nutcracker from Mrs. Cavanaugh, my hands trembling a little. I dance.

Nothing happens.

I stumble, and Mrs. Cavanaugh pauses the music. Instead of critiquing me, she just sighs and clicks the button. "Again."

But I don't go away this time either. Where is he? What's happening? Am I too late?

We have to start over a few more times—I keep making mistakes. I'm rattled. I never gave him my answer. What if I missed my chance? What if he needed my help right that minute, and it's too late now?

We finally finish rehearsal, and Mrs. Cavanaugh closes the Nutcracker up in his wooden box. I stare at it, confused.

I need to tell someone about this. Someone who will believe me and know that this is serious. I need to talk to Kaitlyn.

# 6

I **say goodbye to Justin** and follow Ally up to the dressing room. A group of older girls are there, getting ready last minute for company class. They smile at us in that way older girls do—like they know something we don't—and run out, still gossiping, clouds of vanilla body spray trailing behind them.

Which leaves me and Ally.

I sit on the floor next to my bag. The dressing room is big, divided into four sections separated by rows of open wooden cubbies painted white. Each section has a long bench in the middle, scratched and scuffed, with dancers' names carved in it, all the way back from when Mrs. Cavanaugh started the school. The company and junior company girls mostly take the cubbies, so I leave my clothes and bag in a corner on the carpet. It's safe enough with only my clothes. I know better than to leave anything valuable or sweet in the dressing room, or it'll disappear.

Even though Ally's only a year older than me and not in the junior company yet, she uses one of the cubbies in the first section. Her dad's the accountant for the dance school, and I know—everyone knows—that her family donates a lot of money. But today she grabs her things and comes and sits on the bench where I am. She doesn't start changing. She just sits there, clothes in a pile next to her, looking down at me. Hands in her lap.

Weird. I take off my shoes, but I'm not going to undress with her staring. "What?"

"I'm surprised they picked you," she says. "I'm trying to figure out why they did."

"Because I'll be good at it?" I know I was good at the audition, at least.

She crosses her arms. "Will you?" She wears mascara, which looks funny on her, her lashes black and clumped. It does make her pale eyes stand out, staring down at me. This close up, I can also see a little foundation, slightly too dark for her pink skin.

I wish Kaitlyn were here for this conversation—we could laugh about it later. Kaitlyn and I never cared about bullies. We had each other, always.

But now I have to deal with Ally by myself. I shrug. "I'm glad you didn't get to pick."

If she did, would she have chosen Kaitlyn? Or someone else?

"I'm better, you know." Ally pats her bun, which is still perfect even after that long rehearsal. "That's why I'm first cast. I'm the one everyone will see."

That only stings a tiny bit. She *is* better. She's done it before, so she's proven herself. And first cast is more important—she'll be the one in the newspaper, in TV commercials, and on the video. But in the end it doesn't matter if she's better. I'm Clara too.

But was it really me dancing at the audition? Or was the Nutcracker helping me? Did I only get Clara because of that?

No, I've worked for this for years. *And* I'm the one the Nutcracker asked for help. I suppose it's possible he asked Ally too, but I look at her stiff neck, her mouth in a thin line, and I doubt it. I drop my shoes into my bag. "Great. Can I get dressed now?"

"You always could." Ally peels off her leotard, not even caring that I'm there, and I look away. I'm not shy, but I don't *like* undressing in front of people. Unlike the little kids, we don't wear underwear or anything under the leotard and tights, so we have to get undressed all the way before we can dress again. I pretend to be really interested in something in my bag for a minute.

Then I decide this is silly and Mom's probably waiting outside already, so I'd better go. I undress and put my jeans and sweatshirt on, not looking at Ally or anything but the white walls and the Paloma Herrera poster until I'm done.

Ally is still fastening her fancy boots when I push past her. She throws me a look, curious. I'm curious too. I don't understand why she came over just to have that awkward conversation. She returned from Chicago and got the part; she got first cast. We won't even dance onstage together. What does it matter to her if I'm the second Clara?

I decide to ignore her from now on. We don't need to be friends. I certainly wasn't going to ask *her* about the Nutcracker. I need to focus on the part and doing my best. And fixing the situation with Kaitlyn. And figuring out how to talk to the Nutcracker again, how to tell him I'll help.

I head down the stairs, through the empty lobby, and out the door, looking for Mom, but I'm surprised to see Dad's truck there. He reaches across the seat and throws open the passenger door, warmth flooding from the cab like a wave. "Hop in. Your mother's car wouldn't start, and I've got practice in half an hour. You'll have to come hang out with me tonight."

I sigh inside a tiny bit but don't let it show on my face. I hop up into the truck. I'm happy to be with Dad. But football . . . I can't say I'm happy to go to football practice.

**7**

**I** **find my spot on** the bleachers, behind the team so Dad can "see where I am" (though he hardly ever looks—he knows I'm not going to get into any trouble). I'm five rows up, so I'm not overcome by teenage-boy-sweat stench from the players.

I'm not the world's biggest football fan.

I know I should be. Dad played football in high school and college, and even a year with the Detroit Lions before he got cut. He became a professional coach after that. For the past six years he's been the coach of the high school team here, the Rangers. That's all he thinks about most of the time. Football is huge in our house.

Dad makes sure I'm settled and gives me a bag with dinner Mom sent: a chicken sandwich and two mandarin oranges. When I asked Dad if there was any news on Grandpa, his face got tight and he shook his head, bolting down the stairs.

He's really close to Grandpa Reynolds. I try to picture it for a second, Grandpa in the hospital, asleep. But I can't. He's always so big and warm and loud and *alive*.

I try to think of something else. Usually I bring a book or my homework or *something* to do, but I didn't expect to be here. I sit on the hard metal bench, chewing on the sandwich, tuning out the shouts and grunts of the players on the field, and try not to worry about Grandpa.

My mind starts to go over what happened tonight. Not the dance—I already know the dance, and in the next weeks I'll learn it so well it'll become automatic, muscle memory. Instead, I think about the Nutcracker and that room, with everything so massive around me. It's like onstage in the ballet, when Clara shrinks and the furniture and the tree grow around her until she's the size of a toy. That's my favorite part of the show. When I was small, that moment was completely magical. But back then I was safe with Grandpa, watching from the audience.

Now it feels frightening—a world where you're that small. How could I possibly help the Nutcracker, a *real* Nutcracker, get home?

"Georgie!"

I jump, then smile a little when I see who it is. "Noah. Hey."

Noah Waterston, from reading class. I don't think I've actually talked to him since first grade, since that time I chased him down because Kaitlyn dared me to kiss him.

I did kiss him before he squirmed away.

I blush as Noah plops down next to me. He pushes his fingers up through his unruly pouf of curly hair. It's dark brown, exactly the same color as a football.

"Why are you here?" I ask. Then I wince, hoping that didn't sound rude. I just don't ever see other kids here.

"My brother's on the team. Jackson Waterston. Sixty-two, see?" He points, and I see the number 62, but it's just another back on the bench. With pads and helmets, the players all look the same. The skin on his arms shows, though, smooth brown, the same color as Noah's. "My dad's hoping I'll be interested in playing football if I come and watch."

Sounds like my dad. Though he knows I won't ever be a football player. "Do you want to play?"

"Not even a little. I play Little Guy football, though, junior varsity. He says I have to do it until the end of this year to give it a chance." He shrugs. "I'd rather be on my Xbox or in band." His whole face brightens. "Did you know I'm in band at Emerson? I play trumpet. I even got into the ensemble this year!"

"That's awesome!" I can tell he's excited about it. "I don't really know anything about band."

"It's cool," he says. He taps his hands on his legs, like he's drumming. "This year we're doing a Christmas concert, and we're already practicing for it."

Like *Nutcracker*. "Very cool," I say. Then suddenly I don't know what else to say. I smile a little, probably awkwardly, and tap my foot on the seat in front of me, watch the glitter on my shoes sparkle in the stadium lights.

His cheeks flush—he has really round cheeks—and we both turn back to the practice. The quarterback throws a long pass, and we watch it soar across the field . . . forty yards . . . but the receiver fumbles it. Dad yells at the player. I cringe. That's my least favorite part of football.

It's way worse than Mrs. Cavanaugh. She mostly gets quiet and tense when we don't do well. Or snaps at us. But she doesn't yell loud, not like that. Dad says it's part of the game.

A gust of wind blows sideways across the bleachers, and I shiver, huddling deeper into my sweatshirt. Leaves swirl around on the sides of the field. It'll turn cold soon. Though that's part of football too, bundling up and drinking cocoa with gloves on while you cheer.

Noah clears his throat. "You're still doing that dancing stuff, right?" he asks. *Nutcracker?*

"Yes!" I glance at him sideways, surprised he remembered. Then I lower my voice and whisper, like it's a delicious secret. "You know what? I get to be Clara this year. I just got the part."

It feels good to tell Noah. It doesn't feel like bragging at all.

"Wow, that's the star, right?" His smile is lopsided. "I saw it a couple years ago."

"Kind of." I smile back, and my tongue pushes at me to tell Noah more, even though I don't really know him that well. I can't talk to Kaitlyn about anything right now, and

I do want to tell *someone*. He's easy to talk to. "It really is an awesome show. There's a battle scene and everything. With a cannon, and a hot-air balloon at the end. There'll be performances at the Wilson Theater in December, if you want to come."

Did I just *invite* him? What is my tongue doing, exactly? That's not what I meant to say.

He puts his shoes up on the seats too, his scuffed white tennis shoes next to mine, and smiles. "Sweet." We watch a play—a catch this time. "We're playing a piece from *The Nutcracker* for the ensemble. The march. You know, the big famous part everybody knows." He hums it.

"Really?" I shift, processing this new information. *Nutcracker* music. "I like that. There are lots of trumpet bits in *Nutcracker*. The march, yeah. And the battle scene is crazy with them. It's cool that we're both working with the same music."

I get out an orange and peel it in a single piece, popping slices into my mouth one by one. Halfway through I think to offer him a slice, and he takes it. It's good—sweet and juicy.

After a while he opens his mouth, but he shuts it again. Then opens it. "I wanted to say . . . I'm sorry about Kaitlyn. In reading."

I'm quiet for a minute. I couldn't say anything bad about Kaitlyn even if I wanted to. Best-friend rules. But it's really nice of him to try to make me feel better. "Yeah." *It's terrible,* I think. *And it's not fair, and I don't understand it at all.* "Thanks," I say.

We don't say anything after that. We just watch practice, side by side. We share the other orange. I'm aware he's there, of course, sitting right next to me, but it doesn't feel awkward anymore. It's almost comfortable.

I wonder what Noah would say if I told him about the Nutcracker's asking for help and my going to that room. Would Noah think I'm crazy? Probably. Most people would. Maybe I *am* crazy. But I'm tempted, a little, to tell him. We're not really friends, so it wouldn't be that terrible if he decided I was strange and didn't want to talk to me anymore . . . like Kaitlyn. But he listens pretty well.

Before I can work up the courage to say anything,

about the Nutcracker or anything else, Noah's dad comes up the stairs to take him on a Burger King run. Noah nods goodbye, and I do a half wave.

I watch him follow his dad out of the stadium. Smiling, I tap my feet on the railing, feeling a little better, lighter. I really like that Noah is doing something with *Nutcracker* too. It's like we're connected, a tiny bit, by the music and the show.

I try to just think about the dance, the steps, but somehow my mind shifts to Kaitlyn again. I keep seeing her face at the audition after she was cut. Worse, when she told me she didn't want to talk to me. I've never seen her look like that.

My mood sinks again.

I don't even know what part she did get. We've always been the same until now. Every year, dancing our roles together. I feel like part of me has been cut off, and I need to make up with her to be whole again.

I sit there, wrapped in my worries, until it's time to go home.

## 8

It's been two weeks, and Kaitlyn still won't talk to me. Mom said to leave her be for a while and try again next week. *Next week!* Two weeks is like a year in sixth-grade time.

But I don't have a lot of other choices. If she doesn't answer my calls or messages and ignores me in class, I can't force her to talk to me. I've been sitting next to Noah in reading, but it's not the same.

I'm beginning to wonder if she's mad at me for something else, something besides just getting Clara. She hasn't been at dance class either. It feels weird and lonely without her there next to me. We usually whisper between barre exercises, or laugh. With Kaitlyn it's like we're tackling the

exercises together. Without Kaitlyn it makes me feel alone in a room full of people I know.

This afternoon in class Ally decides to stand next to me, probably to psych me out before the Clara rehearsal tonight. I sigh and stretch my leg on the barre, forehead on my knee. I can pretend she's not there. That will work. It's just me and the steps. . . .

"Where's your friend?"

Slowly, I raise my head. "What?"

Ally does a grand plié, her hands on the barre, but throws a glance at me, all innocent. "The one with the round cheeks? Who flopped at the audition?"

I flinch. "You know her name, Ally. It's Kaitlyn."

She raises her eyebrows and sinks down again, bending her knees deeply. "Did she get thrown out for being terrible?" She laughs, low, to herself. "Or realize it herself and quit?"

I drop my leg and rise up on demi-pointe a few times, staring at the wall. I don't answer her. Where *is* Kaitlyn? Not here. That's all that matters.

I ignore Ally for the rest of class, though she keeps watching me. Afterward we run out for water and a bathroom break, but then it's right back into the room for rehearsal.

Tonight it's just the four of us again, the Claras and the Fritzes. We're starting with the Prologue, when Clara and Fritz do a dance of their own before the party. The Nutcracker hasn't been introduced in the show yet, so he isn't here tonight.

It's strange that Clara rehearsal can possibly feel a little flat, but it does, without the possibility of seeing the Nutcracker and that room again. I have so many questions I want to ask. And I want to tell him I'll help him. But tonight it's just dancing, real-life rehearsal. With Ally, who's waiting for me to do everything wrong.

Ally and Caleb go first while Justin and I sit on the floor. Justin fidgets and rocks. Then he starts drumming his hands on the wooden floor, not quite loud enough that everyone else can hear the sound over the music, but I can. When he keeps doing it, I grab his wrists and shake my head at him.

He pouts but stops. One good thing about my family: I have heaps of experience dealing with little kids.

Our turn. Justin and I get up and go to our places. I try not to be nervous.

I can't not be nervous. It feels scarier today, working on a scene I've never done before, a dance I don't know yet. Like Mrs. Cavanaugh is going to be judging harder than she does for the parts I know. Plus, unlike the audition and that first rehearsal, I'm really here. I'm not getting any magical help with dancing.

She starts the music, and Justin and I come in from stage left. We're supposed to be fighting each other over a doll, a hint at what will come later when Fritz steals the Nutcracker. We dance side to side, each pulling one of the doll's arms, tussling.

"Stop." Mrs. Cavanaugh cuts off the music and we stop instantly. "Were you two paying attention to what I asked you to do? To first cast? You're supposed to move *upstage,* toward where the Christmas tree will be." Justin's face pinches, and she gives each of us a look. Not harsh or shaming, but like she expects more from us. "Do it again."

We move off to the left. She starts the music.

We do that part okay, thank goodness. Chassé right, chassé left, do a wide turn together with the doll between us. End at the Christmas tree.

Well, it's mostly okay. The timing is a little off, and she

wants our arms raised higher so the audience can see the doll. We do it again, and again. Then she teaches us the next part while Ally and Caleb watch. I'm supposed to win the doll from Justin, hug it to myself, and do a spin before our parents come in and shoo us away from the Christmas tree. That's it.

Ally and Caleb take their turn and do fine. I watch Ally closely to see if there's anything she truly does better, anything I can pick up from her. I hate it, but she is really good, technically.

But still, Mrs. Cavanaugh has tons of notes for her and me. "Ally, you're too stiff! Georgie, you're too sloppy with your arms."

She's not going to let us get away with good. It has to be perfect.

When we're done, I'm droopy tired.

Ally's mom is waiting on the bench, knitting, like she always is. Caleb's mom is there too. Mine isn't. Joey has her karate lesson, and Dad has practice. Mom said she was going to be fifteen or twenty minutes late.

I change slowly in the dressing room, head downstairs again, and drop my bag on one of the benches. They're old pews, really, with a high curved back you can lean against. I'm the only one in the big lobby, which is strange. During the day it's always bustling with little kids in their glittery tutus, moms and the occasional dad, older girls stretching and eating and waiting for class. Julia's not even here tonight.

I'm hungry, and I need something to pick me up until dinner. I go over to the coffee-and-tea station and pluck a cube of sugar out of the bowl, let the sweetness dissolve on my tongue.

"Boo!"

I spin, my heart thumping painfully in my chest. Justin laughs, a loud, high-pitched little-boy laugh. I guess I'm not the only one here after all.

"Where are your parents?" I snap.

"They're coming at six-fifteen." He grins. "*You* can stay with me."

There goes my big plan of flopping on the bench until Mom comes.

"Sugar!" He shoves his hand into the bowl, takes three or four cubes, and mashes them all into his mouth.

"You're not supposed to take those," I say. Even though I just did *and* it's too late to stop him.

He pokes me in the side, hard. "Tag, you're it!"

He takes off, weaving his way around the furniture, heading for the classrooms.

I'm the oldest one here. I'm the only other one here. Whatever he does, I'll probably be blamed for it.

"Justin! Stop!" I trot after him.

He laughs and darts into the hallway, around the corner so I can't see him. I pick up the pace and run after him. If he goes into the rehearsal room with Mrs. Cavanaugh . . . I don't even want to think about it. I have to keep both of us out of trouble.

I spot him. He went into the first classroom, the one that's used for adult classes. The door's open. He stands in the middle of the room, waiting for me.

"We can't play tag here," I say from the doorway. "Come out to the lobby."

"No, come in here." His blond hair is stuck to his head at the edges, dark with sweat.

"Justin. No."

"Come in here, and then I'll go to the lobby. Promise."

I sigh. I take a step toward him and he shoots past me, back down the hallway. Dad would be upset if his team's defense let somebody by like that.

When I get to the lobby, though, there's no sign of Justin. I guess he's moved on to hide-and-seek. I check the beginner classroom, but he's not there. He must've gone upstairs to the dressing rooms.

I'm tempted to leave him there, but I shouldn't. Who knows what kind of trouble he'd get into. I can just imagine him in the girls' dressing room, messing with everything.

"Justin?" I call as loud as I dare. "Come down."

I hear a giggle, but it's not from upstairs. It's behind me. I turn. Nothing. He could be in one of the bathrooms—I am *not* going in the boys' bathroom, no matter what happens—or behind Julia's desk. But I see the open door, and I *know* where he is. The office.

Oh no.

**I**'ve never been in the office. I've never even been *near* the office. I don't know what Mrs. Cavanaugh would do if she caught either of us in there, but I'm sure it wouldn't be good. She could take Clara away from me.

"Justin, come out. *Now.*"

Giggle.

I edge closer to the door. "Justin!"

He's gone quiet, which is bad.

I brave it, push the door open, and stick my head in. He's standing in front of an open cupboard, staring up.

"What's that?" he asks, pointing.

"Get out of here!" I whisper. I take a quick look around. It's a normal office, a desk and chair and filing cabinets and a computer—except for the big wooden cupboard he has

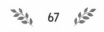

open. It's dark wood, gleaming with polish, with swirls of knots that look like faces. He's standing on his toes, trying to reach a box on a shelf that's a little too high. "I mean it, Justin!"

He ignores me. He gets his fingers on it, whatever it is, but loses his balance. I see it happening as if it were in slow motion: him falling back, the beat-up wooden box sliding down after him.

The Nutcracker box.

I leap for it without thinking and catch it in my arms. I land on top of Justin with an *oof,* but I have it. Safe, I hope.

Good catch. Dad would like that one.

"Ow!" he whines. "Get off me!"

I slide off, cradling the box. I want to check whether the Nutcracker is okay, then put him back. But I don't want Justin in here when I open the box. Never trust a Fritz with the Nutcracker. It's Clara's main rule.

Maybe I can tie Justin to something sturdy until his parents come.

I give him a push toward the door. "Go. And *stay in the lobby.* Your parents should be here any minute."

"But—"

"Go!" I say, and give him the big-sister look that even works on Joey. I close the door behind Justin.

I run my fingers over the writing on the lid, just as Mrs. Cavanaugh did. It's in Russian, I think, beautiful, sharp letters. I wonder what it means.

Carefully, the wood rough against my fingers, I pry up the edge. I'm going to peek to make sure Justin didn't break the Nutcracker, then put him back.

He is there, just as he was, the big head, the black eyes watching me. Not cracked or anything. His mouth, with those big yellow teeth, looks wider than before, like he's really smiling.

Excitement floods through me in a rush, and I know, clearly, what I felt as soon as I saw the box. I'm not going to put him back on the cold, lonely shelf. I'm going to dance with him and see if it happens again. Maybe I can answer him this time.

I reach into the box, lift him out, and hold him in my arms. I feel like excitement and calm curled up together.

I sway and take a few tiny steps to the left.

A dizziness hits me, and I close my eyes, unsteady. When I open them again, I'm not in the office anymore, and my arms are empty.

I'm alone.

The room is the same: the dark wood floor, the candles, the furniture that's far too big. The candles seem farther away, darkness pooling thickly in the corners. I wonder if it's always night here, or if daylight ever shines through the massive window.

I'm standing in front of a cabinet with a glass front, the reflection reaching up as far as I can see. I'm suddenly nervous. I step forward into a stretch of light until I can see myself. I'm wearing Clara's clothes again, the rich nightgown, the soft ballet shoes. My hair is heavy on my back, curled in ringlets.

"Hello?" I call, my voice echoing. "Nutcracker?"

I hear something in the distance. It's a small sound. Skittering.

"Hello?" I whisper.

The sound repeats, louder. It sounds like a dog skritching its nails across the floor. No, more than one dog.

I see a shape on the far side of the room. Huge, stooped. Creeping sideways toward me. And another shape behind it.

It's not until they move across a spark of light that I see the patchy gray fur. The paws curled in front, with long, curved claws. The pointed noses and sharp teeth, the whiskers twitching as the creatures look at me, their eyes glittering hungrily.

These aren't adults in costumes, which are scary enough. These are giant mice, and they're *real*.

I close my eyes, then open them again, wishing to go home. But I'm still here. The mice are advancing slowly across the floor.

I look around. There are no weapons to fight them with. I start to back up, step by step. "Nutcracker!" I yell. "Help!"

But no one is here except me and the mice, and I don't know how to get home. There's a third mouse now, even bigger than the others, with a circle of black around his eye.

My back hits the cabinet. I reach behind me and feel the glass, smooth and slick against my outstretched fingers. I don't want to turn away from the mice, but I do, fast, to see if I can spot anything in there I can use. Or if I can get the front open and barricade myself in it until they go away.

This close, I can see inside for the first time. I'm facing a row of stone-faced, unmoving soldiers. Toy soldiers, like in the show, except these are all the same height, taller than me. Their eyes are open, staring straight ahead. When I look carefully, they seem real, not like toys, but it's as if they're frozen or asleep.

There's no latch on the glass doors, as far as I can tell— though I couldn't reach it if there were.

What was the poem the Nutcracker said? It ties in to the soldiers somehow. Soldiers, battle . . . battle!

*One battle ended,*
*Two links forged,*
*Those who are lost shall be found.*

I check behind me. The mice are close, only a stage-length away. One of them squeaks, high and long, and I shiver. I hear more skittering in the distance.

Well, the soldiers aren't lost. But maybe they're needed for the battle against the mice.

I bang on the glass as hard as I can. "Wake up! Wake up now! I need your help!"

They don't move, their faces unchanging. I bang again, desperate. "Wake up! They're coming! They're going to get me!"

I hear voices, a low murmur, then a boy's voice, high. Whining.

I'm in the office again, holding the Nutcracker in my arms. The mice, the soldiers, and the room are all gone. I hear Justin's mother, then the creak of the outside door. Then quiet.

I set the Nutcracker back in the box, shut the lid, and push it back up onto the high shelf. I close the cupboard and let myself out of the office as carefully as I can.

It seems strange to be in the studio again after that. To have everything be quiet and normal, my bag untouched on the bench. I sit, my legs shaking, and pick at a torn thumbnail. I don't know when I tore it—maybe catching the box? The faint music for the snowflake dance drifts from the studio, all flutes and violins. I've always liked that scene. It feels like a spell, as if the music, the snowflakes and everything, are really transporting you to a different land.

But I *was* in a different land, a dangerous one. I don't know what happened to the Nutcracker, but I do know that I didn't help anything at all.

**10**

A few days later, Kaitlyn is waiting for me outside the cafeteria. Just seeing her there, I feel a burst of pure relief. We're okay again. We can go back to normal, hanging out, doing all our things together. The only difference will be that I'm rehearsing for Clara, but I can talk to her about it at least. And I can finally tell her about the Nutcracker and what's been happening. She can help me figure out what's going on, what I should do next.

When I get to where she's standing, I want to hug her just for being there. I tug on my backpack strap instead and smile.

She doesn't smile back. Her face looks wrong when it's serious. It's round, and she has all those freckles. It's the kind of face that's meant to look cheerful.

She doesn't say anything for a while and just stares at me. My stomach clenches slowly, like it knows something's wrong first.

"Er . . . hi," I say finally. "What's up?"

She frowns. "How's your grandpa? I haven't heard, since we weren't really talking."

"Oh." That's not what I was expecting at all. "No change. He's still unconscious. I can't see him yet."

She nods, bites her lip. "I'm sorry." She takes a deep breath and taps her fingers on her jeans. "But . . . okay, I have something else to tell you. I quit ballet."

I freeze solid. I don't think I even breathe.

She doesn't move either, except for taking one big swallow. And her eyes blinking. Watching me.

I want to rewind the last couple of seconds and start again so it makes sense. My brain just doesn't understand.

"What?" I manage, almost a whisper. "But . . . you can't."

"I did. My mom called Mrs. Cavanaugh. For real. I'm not in *Nutcracker,* or class, or anything. Not anymore."

The warning bell sounds—two minutes to get to first period. It unfreezes me. We turn together, automatically, and start walking. I feel like I'm pushing through mist. "But we've always danced together," I say, helpless. It's weird, but this is what Ally predicted last night. She guessed before I did. *"Why? How can you just stop?"*

Her cheeks are red now. She keeps her head down. "Mom and I had a talk. About how ballet fits in with my future and everything. It's so expensive and takes up so much family time. And I'm not going to be a dancer when I grow up. I never was. We know that. So now is a good time to stop."

I frown. "Is she making you quit? That's not right. She—"

"No! She isn't. Mom and I talked about it before. It was going to be my last year anyway."

I stop, and she stops too. Everyone streams around us, like we're rocks in a river. I stare as though I've never seen her before. "You knew you were going to quit before?"

She nods. "I was going to be Clara and then quit next year. But now . . ." She shrugs and looks away, then back. "Why not now? Since I didn't get it. Choir auditions are today after school, so I'm going to try out for choir."

"But you didn't tell me," I say, low. I feel like she punched me in the gut, and I can't stand up straight, can't breathe. We always danced together. Always. Worse, how could she keep that secret from me?

She looks at her shoes again.

"It's okay, Georgie," she says, quieter. "I'm not mad because of Clara. I only was for, like, a day or two. I just . . . once we decided, I didn't know how to tell you."

The bell rings, and she squeezes my hand and runs off to class. Everyone else clears out too. I stand there, stuck and alone in the hallway. The floor stretches out in front of me like the Nutcracker's room, empty. But I can't dance across it. All I can do is blink.

Is she still my best friend if we don't dance together? If she was hiding things from me?

What will ballet be like without her there?

And I didn't tell her about the Nutcracker. I don't know if I can now. It's as if she's launched herself into a different world and barely even said goodbye.

**At lunch I don't** go to the cafeteria. I take my lunch and go sit outside on the steps, alone. Technically, we're not allowed to do that—everyone is supposed to eat in the cafeteria, and you can get in trouble for going somewhere else—but I had to. I can't go in there and sit with her like nothing has changed.

*Everything* has changed.

I can't stand the realization that she always was going to quit and she never told me. It makes me wonder if she was always hiding part of herself from me, while I was giving her all of myself. I didn't even know she was interested in choir. How could she decide with her mom just like that to stop ballet? How could she not tell me about it until after it was done?

I feel like I don't know her at all, like she's a different person taking Kaitlyn's place. If this were a movie, I would be the only one who could tell this girl was an impostor, and I'd have to fight to get my Kaitlyn back.

I want *my* Kaitlyn back.

I eat a ham sandwich as I look out over the lawn that stretches to the band building and the gym. The grass is still green, but just barely, the tops of the blades fading away to pale brown. Summer fading away to fall.

I wonder if she would've quit if I hadn't gotten Clara. Is it a punishment the universe is handing me? Or a trade? It's like the universe is saying, "You can have the part you always wanted, but in return you'll have to give up your best friend."

Fat tears hit my sandwich, and I shove the rest back in the bag. I'm not hungry anymore.

When the bell rings, I sit there until the last possible minute. Then I take a deep breath, pull on my backpack, and go to reading.

Kaitlyn looks up when I come in, but I don't look back. I veer to the side, keeping my tear-blotchy face turned away, and sit in the empty seat next to Noah.

"Hey," I say brightly when he sees me.

"Hey," he says, and smiles. He's reading *Five Kingdoms*. I just finished that book, about a bunch of kids who disappear into a magical land.

Like me. Kind of.

Neither of us says anything else for the whole period. We just sit there reading our books. I never look to the other side of the room at all.

# 11

**The next day is Saturday.** Usually Saturday mornings are fun, but Dad was super quiet this morning, staring at his cereal. For long stretches he forgot to eat, looking down into the milk as if he didn't know what it was. He didn't say a single word to any of us, even when Joey and Pip were chasing each other around the kitchen, screaming.

His team lost the football game last night. That makes three in a row. I wonder if they're losing because Dad's upset about Grandpa.

Dad's going to the hospital today. I want to go with him, but even if the hospital would let me see Grandpa, I can't; I have rehearsal all day.

Today is the party scene rehearsal . . . with almost the

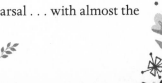

whole cast. There's a pile of party children already there when I arrive. That was my role last year. There are teen dancers too, playing the guest parents. Then there are me and Justin and our "parents," David and Liz. Later the bear and the doll will come for their solo parts, though they're not here today.

However, the Prince is. There's only one this year, playing both casts. We don't have any boy dancers at our studio who are the right age and who are good enough to dance the part. The one who did it the past two years moved away, and nobody good tried out this year, so Mrs. Cavanaugh had to find a boy from another studio. It's the first time I've seen him.

I stand just inside the rehearsal studio door, watching. He's tall, a good foot taller than me. Maybe fourteen? He has a biggish nose that curves out like a beak, and black eyes that slant up at the corners. His hair is black too and flops over his forehead, the opposite of his stark-white skin. With his white shirt and black shorts, he's all black and white, like an old-time movie.

The Prince and Clara do a big dance at the end of the first act, partner dancing, and spend the whole second act together, mostly sitting on a double throne onstage watching the dances in the Kingdom of Sweets. I hope we'll get along.

He sits on the floor and stretches. He'll have to lift me and everything. It'll be so strange doing that with someone I don't know. Well, anyone. I've never done partner dancing before.

Ally struts right over and talks to him. I should introduce myself, like she did. I have as much right as she does, and I should meet him too.

But then I see the box, right there on top of the piano. It's so familiar now, the writing something I could almost understand if I tried hard enough. I want badly to walk over, take off the lid, and free the Nutcracker, dance with him, to see what happens next . . . even with the terrible mice. He probably needs my help against the mice.

I know I can't. I don't dare.

But if the Nutcracker is here, we're almost certainly going to dance with him today. Excitement thrums through me. Something will happen. I don't understand it, but that other place, that echoing room, is calling to me. It's going to happen today; I can feel it.

A hand drops on my shoulder. "How's my darling niece today? Ready for your party?"

I jerk away and look up. Drosselmeyer. Or at least the man playing Drosselmeyer.

He's a parent of a dancer who was here a few years ago. She's in college now, but he still returns to play Drosselmeyer every year. His real name is Mr. Rodriguez. He has wild clouds of white hair and bright green eyes, and he's outrageously tall and skinny, like a scarecrow. Or a skeleton. You can see his cheekbones right there under his skin. When he's in costume, he wears an eye patch.

He's my personal version of creepy. But he looks perfect for the part. Drosselmeyer's meant to be creepy.

He waggles his thick eyebrows. "Oh, did I scare you? So sorry." He grins like he's not sorry at all and sticks out a hand. "You are a Clara, aren't you? I'm Adam Rodriguez. But you can call me Uncle Drosselmeyer. It seems easier."

I tentatively put my hand in his. It's dry and papery. "I'm Georgie," I say, in a voice that seems small even to me. He nods, then wanders off to say hello to Ally. She turns to him happily, as if he really is an uncle. The Prince gets up, pointing his feet.

My gaze drifts back to the box. Then I sigh and make myself move toward the Prince.

"Hello," I say. Again the small voice. I force it to be louder, stronger. "I'm Georgie Reynolds, the other Clara."

He smiles, a little tightening of the lips, without showing his teeth. *"Privyet,"* he says with a strong accent. "That means 'hello' in Russian. I am Peter."

Mrs. Cavanaugh claps her hands, and the room falls to silence. Mrs. Cavanaugh tilts her head. "Hello, everyone. I'd like you all to welcome our Prince for this year. Peter Fyodorov is from Saint Petersburg, but he's spending this year here with relatives, doing an exchange. He's an accomplished dancer, and we are very, very fortunate that he is able to join us for this show." She gives everyone in the room the trademark Mrs. Cavanaugh glare over the top of her glasses. "I expect you to help him as much as you can."

He winks at me, and I almost laugh. Then he does a full bow to the room. Old-style. I could easily believe he's secretly a prince, hidden among the peasants in America for his own safety.

"Now," says Mrs. Cavanaugh, "let us get to work."

We go over the scene, piece by piece, from the beginning. We start with first cast, Ally and Caleb, and then move on to second cast, with me.

In the opening, my "mother," Liz, fusses with my imaginary dress and stands me next to her so I can help greet the guests, before turning to Justin and straightening his tie. As soon as the first guest family comes in, I pull the girls—Lissa and Malia—over to the other side of the stage, where we pretend we're talking and comparing our dresses.

The party scene is supposed to be bouncy and happy, like a real party. It's especially fun for me as Clara because everyone pays attention to me; Clara is the center of everything. We start with a dance where all the kids hold hands and skip in a circle while the adults do a big waltz in the middle. Justin's with me for that part. I whirl to the music, faster and faster, the air cool on my cheeks.

Mrs. Cavanaugh yells, "Stop!"

The music cuts out and everybody tenses, waiting to see who did something wrong enough to stop the rehearsal. This time it was one of the grown-ups.

Whew. I squeeze Justin's hand. It wasn't us.

We do it again, moving step by slow step through the scene. This time we make it past that part, all the way through the dance to where Drosselmeyer enters. The music changes there. It turns imposing and slow as Drosselmeyer hobbles in with his nephew, also played by Peter, behind him. We're almost to it, the part where Drosselmeyer gives Clara the Nutcracker. I feel my nerves jumping, twitching, ready. . . .

"Let's take a break here," Mrs. Cavanaugh calls. "Half an hour, everyone."

I almost groan out loud but manage to remember where I am. Like everyone else, I grab a granola bar from the basket, and then I sit on the bench with Lissa and a couple of other girls. Lissa ended up being a first-cast flower in the Waltz of the Flowers and a second-cast party girl.

"You're doing really good," she says, kind of shy.

I glance at her quickly while I'm tearing open the granola bar wrapper. She seems serious. "Thanks!"

She leans over so no one else can hear. "I'm glad I'm with you and not Ally. She only has her certain friends. She just glares at everyone else."

I laugh loudly. It's true.

"Where's Kaitlyn?" Lissa asks. "I heard she quit when she didn't get Clara?"

I mumble something, not really an answer, and retie my pointe shoes so I won't have to talk anymore.

Mostly I wait . . . and wait and wait. The break is the longest half hour of my life.

Finally it's time to go back in. But instead of picking up where we left off, Mrs. Cavanaugh makes us run through the scene again from the beginning, both casts. I wish I had something that would make time move faster, a fast-forward button.

But then we're there. I hold my breath as Mrs. Cavanaugh opens the box and hands the Nutcracker carefully to Mr. Rodriguez. "Let's do second cast first on this one," she says casually, and I beam.

She shows everyone else what to do—mostly just act in the background—and looks at me. "You know this scene, right, Georgie?"

I nod, my throat dry. I know it. We went over it a dozen times this week. And even if I didn't, would it be me dancing anyway?

The music starts, a little earlier than where we started

during Clara rehearsal. Drosselmeyer gives a trumpet and sword to Fritz, then points to me. I run to him, my feet almost but not quite tripping to get there. I reach up and take the Nutcracker in my arms. I walk back to my place, my arms trembling, as my music begins. . . .

# 12

I'm there, in the giant room. I stand and look around me, inhaling the sweet pine scent, but only for a moment. I don't have much time. I have to find the Nutcracker and figure out how to help him.

The cabinet is still there, a glass tower stretching toward the sky, the soldier army sealed inside it. No one else is here, not even the mice. I'm glad for that, at least.

I move around the cabinet, and for the first time I see a door in the far wall. It's white, standing open a little, throwing a wedge of flickering light on the shiny floor. Good thing it's open. I'd never have been able to reach the doorknob, far above my head.

I run for the door, slipping across the slick wood. I hesitate in the shadow, fear touching me at the thought of

90

those mice. But I have to go through now. I have no idea how long I'll be here, and I have to find him. Maybe that's what the poem means, that he's lost and I have to find him.

This room is smaller, the candlelight brighter. It's some sort of side room, just a huge square with chairs in a line along the walls, a mirror high up, and a shut closet. There's another door on the far side. This room smells musty and old in a way the big room doesn't. I step in farther, around the corner of the door.

I gasp. The Nutcracker is there, standing stiffly, imprisoned in a glass case that fits tightly around him. Like a doll on display in a store. He can't move, and I can't see a hinge or any way to open the case. It's horrible. A glass prison, like the one that trapped Snow White.

I have to get him out of there.

I take a step forward, then shrink back as something else moves, its grotesque bumpy shadow looming ahead as it comes through the other door.

Instinctively, I hide around the corner. The thing scuttles across the floor haltingly, making its way toward the Nutcracker. It comes close enough that I can see it clearly, and I press my hand over my mouth so I won't scream.

It's a mouse, like the others, but so much worse. He's larger and taller than the other mice, with a round belly that wobbles as he moves. The fur is the same, gray and patchy, the yellow claws waving. But the heads . . . impossibly, he has three. Three mouse heads sprouting from the same neck, each one terrible, with glittering eyes and gnashing teeth. On the middle head is a towering golden crown, with smaller crowns on the other two. The Nutcracker stares at him bleakly, still stuck with that endless grin.

I back up as far as I can, only the top of my head peeking around the door so I can still see. There's nowhere to run if the Mouse King spots me.

He stands in front of the Nutcracker in his glass cage and howls, a high-pitched squeak of victory.

"Stop there." I blink, and the room and the horrible thing are gone. Around me is just a circle of dancers, the women all in black leotards and pink tights, the men in white and black. They swirl together, and I think I'm going to faint.

"Georgie," Mrs. Cavanaugh says sharply. "Are you all right?"

I blink again, trying to clutch the Nutcracker to my chest, but I don't have him. Justin's standing over him across the stage, his foot next to the Nutcracker's head, like he smashed him. I make a low noise under my breath before I remember that he's supposed to do that. It's part of the scene.

I blink again, rub my hand hard across my face, and nod. "I'm fine."

She studies me intently, hands on her hips. Then her gaze softens suddenly, like she's not looking at me anymore at all. I see the moment when she gathers herself and returns her focus to me. "Hmmm. Yes. That was very good, Georgie." She turns to Justin. "Fritz, however. My dear Justin, you don't have to be quite so rough with him. It's pretend, you know." Her voice is gentle. She glances at me again, then back to Justin. "And he is precious to me. Be careful, please."

Does she know something? It's her Nutcracker. The way she looked . . . I wonder if she has some idea about the magic.

Justin nods, wide-eyed, and I wait, flexing my fingers. Are we doing it again? Am I going back?

"Let's try it with first cast," Mrs. Cavanaugh says. She looks at the big clock on the wall. "And then I think that will be all for today."

I sit on the floor, numb, and watch Ally do the dance. I'm only half there, trying to make sense of what I saw. Though I guess it's pretty clear what happened. The Mouse King captured the Nutcracker and imprisoned him in that glass case. I wonder if that's what he did with the soldiers too, locking them up in the cabinet. Maybe that's why they didn't move before. It's some kind of magic.

How can a battle be won if they're all locked up already?

If I'm being honest, I don't want to go back there and see the Mouse King again, ever. I have a feeling he would eat me in a second, or lock me up too. I try to imagine what that would be like, sealed in glass, watching but unable to move. A doll, but alive. The Nutcracker's face was so sad, locked away, helpless. . . .

I feel a scream in my chest, aching to get out. Or tears.

I have to go back. That must be what he needed me for, to prevent this, or to rescue him if he was taken. I agreed to help him. I feel the need, deep inside me, to return. I have to save him, open the cage and free the soldiers. I don't know how—all I have are brief flashes of rehearsal time to do it. But it's clearly what I have to do. I look at the small version of him, cradled in Ally's arms as she dances, before Caleb rips him away and runs across the room between the dancers, pretending to smash him on the floor.

The Nutcracker is waiting for me, calling to me. I have to save him.

# 13

**I call Kaitlyn during** the long stretch of Sunday when there's nothing to do but homework. I'm convinced I could fix everything if we just tried harder and had a normal conversation. If I could talk to her about something besides dance, maybe Grandpa or videos or . . . whatever she wants to talk about, like choir.

As her phone rings I practice what I'm going to say. I'm going to be casual and friendly. We can get back to where we were, even without ballet. She reached out to me by telling me about quitting. I'll reach back, just a little late.

Kaitlyn's mom answers. "Hi," I say, as easy as I can. "Is Kaitlyn there?"

"Is this Georgie?" she snaps.

Tension floods in again. "Yes," I say. My voice shakes. "Please. I need to talk to her."

"She's out with friends," her mom says. It feels like she's saying *Of course she's with other people* and *Why are you even calling?* I hang up and almost cry again. The only thing that stops me is that Joey comes in at that moment carrying Ginger all wrong, and I have to rescue the cat from her clutches.

Then I focus on dinner. Sunday is the one night of the week when none of us have activities, so we all have dinner together, even Dad. Which is good. I want to ask him if I can go to practice again this week so I can talk to Noah.

It feels weird to be planning to see Noah instead of Kaitlyn. But I desperately want someone I can *talk* to. Maybe not about the magic stuff, if it doesn't feel right, but about everything else. Someone safe, who won't abandon me afterward. Kaitlyn isn't that for me anymore.

I set the table while Mom finishes cooking. She always seems stressed about cooking on Sundays. It's as though if we're all together she has to make fancy stuff, and it has to be like it's from a cooking show, perfect and laid out pretty and everything. Tonight she's making pesto pasta, one of my favorites, but she's muttering at the pot. I do my best to stay out of her way when she mutters.

Joey wanders in with an empty glass in her hand and bumps into Mom, splattering green sauce on the counter.

"Joey!" Mom snaps. "Please pay attention to where you're going!"

Joey doesn't say anything, not even "sorry," but makes a face and starts to head back out, glass still empty. I grab her arm. "You saw Dad tonight when he came home," I whisper. "How is he?"

Her eyebrows go up. "Very Dad-like." She shrugs. "Normal."

Good.

When dinner's ready I get to call everyone in, and we all take our seats. Dad picks up the big bowl of green-sauced pasta—bow ties that I chose at the store—scoops himself some, and passes it around. He's not zombie-sad like yesterday, but he still doesn't seem happy. His forehead has two lines in it, right in the middle.

I'll have to cheer him up.

"Dad," I start. He looks up, his eyes crinkling at me. "Can I go to football practice with you on Monday again, after rehearsal? And maybe some of the other days?"

His eyebrows come down, and the lines get a little deeper. "Why would you want to do that, Georgie-Porge?"

I wish he wouldn't call me that. It's so babyish.

I shrug. "I thought it was fun last week." He doesn't look convinced, so I talk more. "It was nice after all the rehearsal stuff to just relax and hang out and watch you."

True, actually. And to talk to Noah.

He looks at Mom, and they have one of those silent conversations. He smiles a little. "Sure. We can do Mondays and Wednesdays, after your rehearsal. That works."

"I want to come too," Joey says.

*"No!"* I say immediately. Joey can't come. How will I talk to Noah or relax even a little? She'll spy on us, and she'll tell everyone . . . I don't know what she'd say. I'm not planning anything she can tattle about. But Mom and Dad both give me the *look,* like I was oh so rude.

"I'm the one who likes football," Joey says, pouting. "She doesn't even understand football. I want to come."

"You can come too, kiddo," Dad says easily. "But your sister has to watch you." He narrows his eyes at me. "You know I won't have time."

Joey beams, probably just because she messed up my plans. I sigh, but I don't argue. It wouldn't change anything. Great. Now I'm going to have to hang out with Noah with my interfering little sister right there.

"That gives you a chance to go to the hospital if you want to," Dad says to Mom. "Grandma could watch Will and Pippa if you want to say hi to Grandpa. It would give her a nice break."

"Is Grandpa awake?" I ask, gripped with the sudden hope that he's okay and they just haven't told us.

"No, honey," Mom says. "He's still asleep."

The hope flattens, like a soda can smashed with your foot.

"I'll go," she says to Dad. "That's a great idea."

He nods. He looks older, more tired, than he did even a couple of minutes ago.

Mom tells a story about what Will did today, sitting up against the pillows watching *Sesame Street* with Pippa, and I'm glad we're talking about something else.

After dinner I lug the trash out to the cans without even being asked. It's dark and cold outside, and the bag is heavy.

I hear a high-pitched sound and a rustle, and I spin. I think of the Mouse King, that terrible shape skittering across the room.

I peer into the darkness, but I can't see anything except trash cans and grass. He couldn't follow me here, right?

It comes again, closer. That was definitely a squeak. I take a step backward, trembling. Then there's a thump and a crash, and I nearly fly out of my skin.

Ginger shoots past my legs like she's chasing something, and disappears down the alley.

It was the cat. I breathe, my heart returning slowly to normal again. When I turn back around, the house is waiting for me, all bright with light spilling out the windows. I stand and look at it for a second, the warmth. What is the Nutcracker's home like, the one that he wants to get back to?

The door opens, the light shining in a triangle like the door in the Nutcracker world. "Georgie?" Dad calls. "You okay? Come in—we're going to play Crazy Eights."

"Coming," I say quietly.

I can't help Grandpa, but maybe I can help the Nutcracker get home instead.

**On Monday, Kaitlyn and I** ignore each other even more than before. Every time I see her, I close my eyes and try to think about the Nutcracker instead, trapped in the glass box. I can work on that. There's someone who actually wants to talk to me. He *needs* me.

In reading class I sit with Noah again. He's still reading *Five Kingdoms*.

"Do you like that?" I whisper. "I just read it too."

"Are you kidding?" he says, almost too loud. "It's awesome. It's my favorite kind of book: magic, other worlds, battles . . . and the floating castles! I've already got the next one on hold at the library."

I grin. He loves magic too. And other worlds. He really might get it. "I'm going to be at practice tonight. Are you?"

His eyes get really bright, but he just nods. "See you there."

• • •

**At rehearsal I'm surprised** that the Fritzes aren't there . . . but Peter, the Prince, is. Me, Ally, and Peter. No Nutcracker box.

Mrs. Cavanaugh smiles. I think she's pleased she surprised us. "Tonight, my dears, as Peter is here, we will start with the partner work at the end of the first act."

From that moment, I don't have a second to think about the Nutcracker. I have to concentrate hard on the dance. Ally knows it already—she did it last year. But this is my first attempt at partner work. Peter has to *lift* me.

Luckily, I fall only once.

Mrs. Cavanaugh is right—Peter is a very good dancer. It's a simple dance, really: some solo bits, then we meet up and he spins me in a pirouette (his hands on my waist!) and keeps his hands there to balance me for an arabesque. I catch a glimpse of us in the mirror, one leg stretched out straight and long behind me, my pointe shoe in a good arch against the floor, with him holding me steady. I feel suddenly grown up, like a real dancer.

All those parts of the rehearsal are fun, if awkward. It's the lift that's so strange. My right leg is still straight out behind me, like it should be in arabesque . . . and he's supposed to lift me up into the air. Then I bend my left knee and move my arms ("Gracefully!" Mrs. Cavanaugh calls), and he tips me forward in what is meant to be a beautiful dive.

It's scary, even though he's strong. My face is only a foot from the floor. The first time I panic as soon as he lifts me off the ground, lose my balance, and fall forward. Mrs. Cavanaugh doesn't even speak, just tightens her mouth and gestures for us to try again. The second time we do it successfully, though I know it looks bad. Not graceful in the least. Ally smirks.

"Very well," Mrs. Cavanaugh says with a sigh when I stand up, my cheeks hot, Peter still close behind me. "We have plenty of time to work on it. That will be all for tonight. Partnering again on Wednesday."

Her words hit me like a tackle. If we don't use the Nutcracker on Wednesday, it'll be at least Saturday before I can get to him again. A full week trapped in the glass prison . . . unless the Mouse King has done something worse to him by then, killed him outright. I can see him so clearly in my mind, his desperation, like he's reaching out for me. I can't wait that long.

I'm dying to talk to someone about this, to bounce ideas off.

I wonder if I can talk to Noah tonight. I think maybe I can.

# 14

**I actually forgot that Joey** would be coming to football practice until I get in the car and see her there, arms folded, looking out the window. Right.

"Hey-ho," Dad says. "Let's get moving!" He gives a thin smile, but there are still creases between his eyes.

I jump into the truck next to Joey. "Anything on Grandpa?" I whisper under the sound of the engine.

She shakes her head. "No change," she whispers back. "They were talking about it after Grandma called."

I bite my lip and trace my finger down the cold window.

As soon as we get to the stadium, Joey and I take our places on our bench, and Dad heads down to his boys. Noah isn't here yet, though I see Jackson with the team.

"I'm hungry," Joey whines after five minutes. "I want a hot dog. And popcorn."

I frown at her. "Didn't Mom give you dinner for us?" I notice for the first time that she doesn't have a bag.

She stares hard at the field.

"Joey," I say sternly, "where's our dinner?"

She shifts, pulling on a strand of her hair. "Maybe Mom forgot it."

"*You* forgot it, you mean."

She doesn't answer. Which means she did. It's probably sitting on the counter at home. Or she left it there on purpose, hoping for hot dogs.

"I'm *hungry*," she says again.

I sigh. Me too. "Concessions aren't open, Jo. You know that. They're only for games. And we can't bother Dad once he's running practice." I dig up a granola bar from the bottom of my bag, but that's all I have. We'll have to wait until we get home. "Watch the practice," I say, handing her the bar. "And be quiet. Please."

Still no Noah. Where *is* he? I can't do anything but wait and watch the drills. The players are just running back and forth across the field. Back, forth, back, forth. At least we don't do the same thing over and over at warm-ups. Wait. I think of tendus, pointing our toes over and over. I guess we do.

Twenty minutes later Noah finally comes in with his dad, carrying Burger King bags. He sees me, pauses when he sees Joey, then climbs the stairs anyway. Joey watches him all the way, suspicious.

He stops next to us and stands there, looming, like a small bear. "Hey."

All of a sudden it feels uncomfortable, as though I'm seeing this situation through someone else's eyes. Through Joey's. I know Noah and I are just hanging out together. I wanted—maybe—to talk to him about the Nutcracker (and hope he doesn't think I'm insane). But it could *look* like—kind of—a date.

But it's not.

"This is my friend from school," I tell Joey. "We're . . . um, working on a project together." Noah raises his eyebrows, but he doesn't correct me. "Don't say anything about it, okay?"

"If you give me fries," Joey answers immediately.

I sigh. "They're not for you."

Noah smiles. "I got an extra one for you," he says, and hands over a bag. It smells fantastic, but I pass it to Joey and scoot away from her so she won't hear us. Noah sits. He pulls out another bag of fries and offers it to share. They're hot and salty and perfect, and I lick my fingers after the first one.

"Are you allowed to eat fries?" he asks suddenly. "With ballet and all that. Aren't you supposed to eat only healthy stuff?"

Joey snorts loudly. I guess she can hear us.

I ignore her and shrug. "Mrs. Cavanaugh never says anything about it. Some of the older girls are really careful. Most of the girls I dance with eat a lot of food, though. Junk food and healthy, usually whatever's around or fast. Dancing uses a ton of energy."

"They all eat like pigs, she means," Joey says.

Noah laughs, and I glare at my sister. "I've been working on that project for science," I say loudly, chewing on another fry. "What have you done so far?"

Totally made up, of course. Noah isn't even in my science class.

Noah scoots farther down the bench, away from Joey,

and I scoot after him. The football players have just now stopped running and doing warm-ups and are starting plays. "A project, huh?" he asks. "Did I forget we were working on a project?" He looks a little confused but pleased.

*"Georgie's got a boyfriend,"* Joey singsongs.

Oh my *God*. I turn and hard-glare. "I said don't say anything. Do you want me to take the fries back?"

She shrugs, but she stuffs her mouth full and makes a face at me.

When I turn back, Noah's suddenly interested in his shoes, his cheeks dark.

"I'm sorry," I whisper. "She's horrible."

He glances up sideways. "Little brothers and sisters. My mom says they keep us from thinking too highly of ourselves."

We both laugh. We watch the practice for a while as he eats and shares some of his food, but it's not very interesting. I don't know what to say. It seems dumb now, that I would tell him anything about the Nutcracker. Of course he would think I've lost my mind. Or that I'm just making it up to be strange. No one would get it.

"Is everything okay?" he asks, low.

I glance at him sharply. Why does it feel like he *knows* something?

He studies his shoes again. "I mean . . . with Kaitlyn."

"Oh." I sigh and start pulling the pins out of my bun, one by one. I guess best-friend rules don't apply anymore. "Yeah. I'm not even sure what happened. I got Clara and she didn't, and then she just . . . quit ballet. We've been dancing together since we were six. We've always done everything together, you know?"

He nods. "That's rough."

"Yeah. It's awful." I take a breath but don't look at him. *You can tell him*, I think. *He likes magic books. He'll get it.* "But that's not the reason everything's been so weird, not really."

"Yeah?" He stares at me, his brown eyes bright, interested.

I have to just trust him.

I tell him. Once I start, I can't stop. I tell him everything, from the audition to the Mouse King, the mice, the soldiers, the Nutcracker trapped in the glass cage. I even tell him about the riddle poem, about the battle and the links and finding what was lost. I check once or twice to make sure that Joey isn't paying any attention, but she's focused on the football. Noah isn't. He listens, and I feel my stress unroll, bit by bit, as I share the details. It's only when I'm done, when I've told it all, that I get a sharp pang of worry. Maybe I've gone too far.

"I know," I say. "It sounds crazy. . . ." I drift off, waiting.

"Yeah," he says, straight-faced. "It does."

My worry balloons. This was a mistake. I was wrong. He'll walk away, and now I won't have *any* friends.

"But here's the thing." He frowns, squeezing his hands together. "My aunt, she has this story she tells." He raises his eyebrows. "Well, she only tells a few people, but she told me. When she was a kid, something strange happened to her one summer, while she was swimming in a lake in Michigan. How she tells it"—he looks at me straight on—"there's another world, under the lake. And she helped the people there. My parents say it's just a silly story, but I believe her. I always have. I believe in magic."

"I do too," I say, almost in a whisper. And I realize right then that I truly *do*. I'm not just going along for the ride with this. I believe in magic. I believe that what's happening is real, not a dream, and that it's critical that I help the Nutcracker. I can't explain it, but I believe it all the way to the tips of my fingers.

"So what if," Noah says, "you forget that it's crazy and move forward assuming that it's real, and you have to respond that way. Right? I mean, it's happened more than once. In books and movies and stuff, if it happens more than once, it's real, right?"

"Right," I say. I'd thought that too. The worry shrivels to nothing. He believes me.

He looks at the field, but I don't think he's watching the players. I look too, thinking.

"What if I borrow the Nutcracker?" I say, almost to myself.

"Borrow it?"

I take a deep breath. I can't believe I'm saying this. Mrs. Cavanaugh said only to touch him in rehearsals. She said to be so careful with him. But I *would* be careful. "The rehearsals don't give me enough time to do anything. What if I borrow him and take him home? Then I could have as much time as I needed to help him break out of the glass cage."

He squeezes his hands together again, then spreads them wide on his knees. "That makes sense. And you said it always stops when you're interrupted. I could be there and pull you out if something goes wrong, or after a certain amount of time."

"I could put him back the next day," I say. "No one would know."

I consider. If Mrs. Cavanaugh ever found out I stole the Nutcracker, she'd not only take Clara away but kick me out of ballet too. Taking him out of the school is *so* against the rules. It's against the law, probably.

But it's the only way I could ever get enough time to save him. If I go in with a plan, and Noah is there to get me out if it's dangerous, I bet I could do it. I *could* do it. It's the only safe way. If we're lucky and everything works, then I could put the Nutcracker back and no one would have any clue at all what happened. And I wouldn't be doing it on my own. Noah would be my anchor.

"Are you sure you would want to help?" I ask. "You aren't part of this. You could get in trouble too."

He pushes up his hair, crinkling it with his fist. "I always listened to my aunt's story and wished and wished something like that would happen to me. If I can help, I will."

I want to hug him, for just a second. I tap my shoes instead. "So what do I do when I get there?"

"That riddle," he says. "'Those who are lost shall be found.' That's the Nutcracker, right? He's lost in the glass cage?"

"Noah!" Noah's dad is standing at the foot of the stairs. "Come down here. I want you to watch this part with me."

Noah groans under his breath, but he stands. "I have to go. We'll find a way to talk about it tomorrow, okay?"

I watch him trudge down to his dad, relief and surprise filling the holes where worry was. I told him, and he didn't dismiss me. He listened. He believed.

"You probably think he's cute, don't you?" Joey says in my ear. I shake my head, ignore her. "Ugh," she says. "He's not cute. He's gross. All boys are gross."

"He's not gross," I snap. "Shut up, Joey. He's my friend."

My friend. He is, isn't he? He really is.

# 15

When I get to school the next day, my brain is tired from running in the same loops. How do I get hold of the Nutcracker without being seen? Once I do, how do I open the glass case? How do I wake up the soldiers? I need a plan. I slog through the crowds out front, my chin up, not paying attention to anyone around me.

But Kaitlyn is waiting at our meeting place. I stop cold. Then I walk up to her, wary.

"Hi," she says shyly.

"Hi," I say carefully, gripping my backpack straps.

"I got into choir!" she blurts out, flashing the Kaitlyn smile I know so well. "Soprano two! Can you believe it?"

"No . . . ," I say. Then, "I mean, that's great."

She starts walking, and I fall in next to her, like I used to.

"Rehearsals start tomorrow, and we're going to do a big concert at Christmas and everything. It's so much fun! See?" She skips. "My mom said everything works out the way it's supposed to. This is probably what I was supposed to be doing, Georgie. You can do ballet, and I can sing."

"Yeah," I say slowly. I feel like I'm a step behind. Are we just going back to the way we were, without even talking about it?

"We can still be best friends, right?" she asks, her voice soft. She links her arm with mine, like we used to when we were six or seven. She doesn't say, *I missed you*, but I think that's what she means. I missed her too. It hurt when she was mad, when she quit ballet, and when she kept me out of what was going on with her. It hurt watching her hanging out with other people. It felt like I was floating around, a lost balloon, without my best friend. More than anything, I want things to be just as they were before. The way I remember things being.

"Yes," I say. "Of course."

I see Noah on the other side of the hall, heading to his first class, and I realize that even if I'm friends with Kaitlyn again, he's the one who knows my secrets now. I can't explain it, but for some reason I don't really want to tell Kaitlyn about the Nutcracker. Not yet, anyway. I guess I don't trust her enough anymore.

Kaitlyn follows my look and narrows her eyes a little.

So *is* Kaitlyn still my best friend if I don't tell her everything? If I'm still a little mad at her for abandoning me? It feels like there's a space between us that wasn't there before.

We sit together at lunch. I listen to her tell me all about choir rehearsal and what they're going to sing, but I have trouble focusing, my thoughts jumping in and out of the conversation. She even asks me if everything's all right. She doesn't ask about Clara or the Nutcracker—but I wouldn't know what to say anyway. We walk together to reading, though, just like we used to.

But when Kaitlyn heads to our spot in the back, I hesitate.

This is a perfect opportunity to talk about the plan with Noah, at least a little. But how can I go sit with Noah when I just made up with Kaitlyn? He sees me and raises his eyebrows, smiling crookedly.

Kaitlyn glances over at him too, then at me standing at the front of the room. She walks back to me.

"What are you doing?" She blinks innocently, but I see suspicion underneath.

I look at Noah again. He never turned on me or kept me out of things. He listened to all the craziness and offered to help, right away.

"I . . . think I might sit over there today."

Her face crumples, and instantly I feel bad.

"I could sit with you tomorrow," I say fast. "I just want to hang out with him sometimes too."

"You like him?" she asks, her voice loud. Too loud. A couple of people laugh. Noah buries his head in his book.

"Shhh!" I step in close to her, my voice low. "It's not like that. We're friends. Come on."

Her eyes blaze. "I've seen you, Georgie. You've been acting strange. And you've been sharing looks with Noah.

Why are you hanging out with *him*? Why wouldn't you tell me that you like him or whatever?" She folds her arms, her face puckered into that hard look again.

I have a huge lump I can't swallow past. I think of all that has been going on, all that she hid. How she wouldn't answer my phone calls. "Why didn't I *tell* you? You weren't even talking to me!" Suddenly anger busts through, and I can't stop the flood. "What was I supposed to do, be alone because you didn't want to talk to me? Not talk to anyone else ever? And you didn't tell me you were going to quit ballet until you already had. You lied to me first."

We stare at each other. The corners of my mouth twitch, dragging down. That wasn't what I wanted to say. Mr. Anderson comes in behind us, takes one look, and clears his throat.

"Maybe we're not really friends, then," she says, quietly.

"Maybe not," I say.

We head to opposite sides of the room. I can feel her watching me. It feels like everyone is watching me. I sit down and make a show of talking to Noah as though everything is normal, though he frowns. He saw it all. Heard it all.

I don't talk to him about the plan. I'm too upset for that. I can't even read. Only one thought keeps spinning around and around, uselessly:

I'm not friends with Kaitlyn anymore.

# 16

**I felt so bad about everything** that I cried in bed last night, quietly so Joey wouldn't hear me. But today it feels like things are going to turn around. There's Clara rehearsal tonight. And football practice, so I can *finally* talk to Noah about the Nutcracker again. I feel good the whole day, like we're going to be able to figure this out.

In rehearsal the bubble breaks, and I plummet back to reality.

We're doing the partner dance again, just as Mrs. Cavanaugh promised. But if I had problems on Monday, I am hopeless today.

I watch Ally first. The solo part of her dance is beautiful, and she and Peter are smooth together. Her arabesque isn't perfect—her standing foot wobbles, and her leg is too low for a good line. But the turns work, and, most important, the lift works. He holds her perfectly in the dive.

Then it's my turn. I stumble through the solo piece first, and Mrs. Cavanaugh makes me stop and start over *four* times. I don't know what's wrong with me. I think maybe I'm too distracted, or maybe it's just an off night. I don't know, but I watch Mrs. Cavanaugh's face get tighter and tighter every time I mess up, and my stomach clenches too.

By the time we get to the partner piece, I'm so flustered and angry with myself that I can't hold the arabesque, even with Peter helping me. I can't turn, and I end up falling into him. We don't even get as far as the lift. My face is red, and I'm almost crying. She could still take the part from me, give it to someone else. Not Kaitlyn, but someone else. Anyone else would do better than I'm doing tonight.

I try not to look at Ally, but I can't help it. Her face has a thousand smug words stamped all over it.

"Enough!" Mrs. Cavanaugh snaps after another fail. I drop my arms, and Peter lets go of my waist, expressionless. She calls me up to her with a crook of her finger. That's it, I think. She's going to let me go, and I won't be

Clara. I won't ever be onstage, and I won't have a chance to save the Nutcracker after all. I let everybody down.

As I stand in front of her, I bite my lip so I won't cry.

"Georgie," she says softly so only I can hear. "I don't know what it is, dear, but it's something." She tilts her head, looking at me. "I think you have a lot going on right now, yes?"

I don't answer, just look at my traitor feet that won't do what I want.

She touches my shoulder. "Go. Take a ten-minute break by yourself. Calm down; have some water. Rest in the lobby. Get yourself together. Then come back and we'll try it again, okay?"

I nod and walk out stiffly without looking at Ally or Peter. I make it to the hallway before the tears escape in a rush. It's not only frustration, though. Relief is stirred in too. She didn't kick me out. She's giving me another chance.

I have to pull myself together.

There aren't any other rehearsals going on right now, or classes, so I'm alone. I wander slowly down the hall-way, hugging my arms tightly across my chest, trying to slow my breaths. I can do this. I hear Dad's voice in my head, the words he says to his players every year, over and over, in practice: *If it was easy, everyone would win. If it was easy, everyone would succeed. You have to choose the path you want, and then overcome the obstacles. You have to make it happen.*

I can do it. I just have to be calm and confident, and it'll be okay.

I head into the lobby and go straight for the sugar bowl. One—no, two pieces. I let one melt on my tongue, the sweet crystals dissolving.

It's only when I turn, the second sugar lump in my fingers, that I realize it.

The lobby is completely empty. I'm alone. And the office door is standing open.

I almost choke on the sugar.

*No,* my sensible brain says before I can consider the possibility. *Not now. You can't steal the Nutcracker now. You don't have a plan. You haven't even talked to Noah yet. What would you do with the Nutcracker tonight?*

I take a step toward the office, then look over my shoulder. There's absolutely no one here. I could dive in there, take him, and hide him upstairs in my bag, and no one would have any idea. He won't be looked for again until Saturday morning. Surely I could figure out what to do, tonight or tomorrow. I could come early on Saturday and put him back.

This is insane. A minute ago I thought Mrs. Cavanaugh was going to throw me out because I was dancing so badly. She *would* throw me out for this. No question. She would be right to.

I step closer, drawn like a magnet. It just feels like the right thing to do, what I *need* to do. And if I'm going to take him, it has to be now. There will be no other chance this good. I've never seen that door open without someone in there.

I think of Dad's words about grasping opportunities.

I look around me one last time, then run into the office. I turn on the lights and pull open the tall cabinet. He's there, shut up in his wooden box. I stand on tiptoe, pulling the box with the tips of my fingers. I catch him when he slides down to me.

I hold the box for a moment, breathing fast, my eyes closed. It's here, now. The point of no return.

I turn off the lights, close the door, and run upstairs to the dressing room. I should have thought to check first, to make sure no one was around to witness me and my stolen treasure. But there wasn't enough time. Thank God the room is empty. I fit the box—barely—into my dance bag and zip it up.

Done. I can't believe I did that, but I have him now. Noah can help me figure everything out tonight.

It's been almost ten minutes since I left rehearsal. I head back, the thrill humming through me. I did it. My mood has completely flipped. I don't think I'll have any trouble with the dance now.

# 17

**I can barely keep my face** straight as I lug the heavy bag carefully to the truck, then up the stairs at the stadium. I still don't know if I did the right thing, but it's done. I have him.

I ignore Joey, and she mostly ignores me. At least she brought dinner this time. Noah isn't here yet, so I sit and wait, the dance bag held tightly between my feet.

When he comes, I practically leap off the bench, waving.

"What are you *doing*?" Joey asks sourly. "Are you crazy?"

"Stay here," I say. "I'm going to talk to Noah."

"I'm not going anywhere. I don't have a *boyfriend* to meet," Joey snaps. "Though I might tell Mom."

I ignore her and heft the bag over my shoulder. I move to a bench across the aisle so she can't possibly hear.

Noah looks amused when he comes up the stairs, a half grin on his face. He pushes one hand up through his hair. "Joey again, huh? I should bring P.J. next time so they can hang out together. Did you think of something?"

"Better." I bounce on the bench until he sits next to me, blocking Joey's view. Then I stealthily unzip the bag and point to the box nestled on top. "I had the perfect chance. I took him."

His face wipes blank. "Wow." He swallows and stares at the box, the writing. He leans over to see it better. "I can't believe you really took it. Wow!" He looks up and smiles a little, his eyebrows high. "So . . . what are you going to do now?"

I zip up the bag again, my fingers shaking. "I have to figure out what to do when I go there. But you'll help me, right?"

"Right." He clears his throat. "Do you have any ideas? How to get him out of the glass?"

I'm quiet. The quarterback throws a long pass, and Noah's brother, number 62, goes out for it. He catches it, holds it for the shortest of seconds, then fumbles. The ball rolls away, and Dad swears. I hear a groan from the stands too—Noah's dad.

"I was thinking," I say, "that I need to break out the soldiers first. In the show, the soldiers come out before you ever see the Nutcracker. Like the front lines? They could help, or distract the mice or something. . . ."

He drums his fingers on the bench, in rhythm. *Tappity-tappity-tap.* It reminds me of Justin. "That's good. Yeah. But how do you get them out?"

"They're in a big glass case," I say. "No latch. I think there must be some magical way of opening it. But he said 'one battle ended' when he was asking me for help. So that's what I need to do, right? Let the soldiers out and end the battle with the mice."

He frowns. "Okay. How do the soldiers come out in the ballet? Maybe it's the same."

I close my eyes and try to picture it. The battle scene begins after Clara has shrunk and the tree-growing music has been playing, up and up, to a crescendo. There's a moment of silence. Then there's one note, then the battle call, almost soft, and the blast of a cannon.

I'd almost forgotten about the cannon. There's a puff

of smoke at the same time the orchestra makes a huge cracking noise.

After that the battle call starts in earnest, trumpets making the same call over and over, with a piping flute.

It hits me, a lightning bolt, and my eyes fly open. "They're called. There's a battle call in the music." I laugh. "I should have thought of it, sitting here with you. It's a big fanfare of trumpets."

"No way." He grins. "Really? It's too bad I can't give you my trumpet to take with you."

"Right? But you can't. I've thought about how it works. Every time it's the same; I go when I dance with him. And once I'm there, I'm dressed in Clara's clothes. I can't bring anything." I shake my head. "And I don't know how to play a trumpet, anyway."

"True. I do, but I'm not the one going."

"I think if I hum it—"

"Hey," Joey says, right next to Noah. "Do you have any fries tonight?"

"Crap, Joey!" I say. "Don't do that!"

"Crap?" Her eyebrows shoot for the sky, and I know I'm in for it now. "Did you just *swear*?"

"Only because you scared me, weasel. Don't tell Mom and Dad."

She narrows her eyes. "What'll you give me?"

I open my mouth to argue.

"I'll bring you fries every time I come," Noah says quickly. "I don't have any tonight, but next time. A whole bag just for you." He sticks a hand in his sweatshirt pocket and pulls out a mini bag of M&M's. "Here, these are for tonight. Now leave us alone, okay? We're working on a project, and we need to concentrate."

She snatches the bag like a monkey and runs back to her spot. I stare at Noah and snort.

"What?" he says defensively.

"That was amazing. Thanks. That may actually work."

He shrugs. "Told you I have a little brother. Bribes almost always work. So . . . you think you need to call the soldiers with music. What do you do when you find the Nutcracker in the cage? Do you call him too somehow?"

I smile. "I use the only weapon Clara ever uses. My shoe."

He laughs, loud. "Of course." Then he stares at the

field for another minute. "So maybe you should go to this place tonight."

Instantly my blood pulses, zinging around my body. I squeeze the bag tighter between my feet, feel the edges of the Nutcracker's box press sharp against my calves. My first instinct is to say no, that I couldn't, not now.

But could I?

"No one's paying attention to us," he says. "I'm here to pull you out of it. You could at least check and see what's going on, right? You think you know what you need to do. Hum the battle call, use your shoe." He grins. "I want to see it happen, see you go to this other place. And there won't be a better time."

I grin back, even though my heart is hammering. With these nerves, I could probably do the biggest jeté in the world. I feel like I could leap across the field.

"Okay," I say slowly. "Let's do it. I know the perfect place." I lift the dance bag onto my shoulder and tell Joey we've got to do something for our project. She doesn't believe me, but it doesn't matter. I don't think we'll be away for long. I'll just go quick and see what's up, and then we can do the full plan next time.

We hike all the way up the steps and then back down around on the left, the back stairs. There's a property shed nestled under the bleachers. It's unlocked during practices and games, while the equipment is out on the field.

I hear Noah clomp behind me, and I turn. It's dark under here, but I can see well enough to make out his expression. He looks way more excited than scared. I'm kind of the other way right now. But then I'm the one who's going. He just has to watch me.

"Here," I whisper when he gets close enough.

"Cool." His eyes shine in the bit of light from the stadium that reaches the shed. "Are you ready?"

"Think so." My hands are trembling. I have to pull hard to unstick the shed door, but I finally get it, and we step inside. I dig a tiny flashlight out of my bag—Dad makes me keep it on my key chain—and shine it around. The place is half-empty, with all the flags and balls and other supplies out on the field. There's plenty of room for us. It's perfect as long as I don't think about spiders. I can hear practice from here, the shouts and crashes on the field. I unzip the bag and lift out the box. I can smell the musty spiciness, intensified in the small space.

Noah stands there, awkward. "You know what you're going to do? Can I help with anything?"

"Not now," I say. "You can come stand over here, though, near enough to snap me out of it if I do something strange or sound scared or anything. Otherwise, ten minutes."

"Got it."

I take a deep breath, suddenly petrified of the mice. But this is safe. Noah can get me out. Ten minutes max. I open the box and shine my little light in. The Nutcracker is there, in perfect shape still, his eyes glittering.

Noah whistles when I pull him out.

"I know," I say. "Creepy, right?"

"This whole thing is a little creepy," Noah says, with a glance around the dark hut.

I take a deep breath, hold the Nutcracker close, and sway. I take a few steps to the right, then to the left. Of course I didn't think about trying to dance in a dark, dirt-floored hut with stuff on the ground.

I feel myself trip like it's in slow motion, the sudden loss of balance, and I know I'm going to fall hard, right on top of the Nutcracker. I hug him tight, to protect him, but something catches me. . . .

Even before I open my eyes, I feel the change of the space around my body. It's wide open now, cool instead of stuffy. The sounds of football are gone. The light dances across my eyelids.

"What the heck?"

I spin, skidding in the slippers, and almost fall again. Noah catches me.

*Noah came with me.*

# 18

Noah is dressed like the soldiers in the glass case: a bright red uniform shirt with round white buttons, white pants, and a bright blue sash across the front. He's wearing a tall black toy-soldier hat with a short brim and a chin strap that looks uncomfortably tight. We use a copy of that hat in the show, but ours are cheap and light. This whole uniform looks heavy, made of good, thick fabric.

He caught me when I fell. That must be why he came—I was holding his arm. I still am. I let go, and he gestures at himself. "What the heck? I wasn't supposed to come."

"You caught me," I whisper. "You were touching me. That must be why. But it looks like you have a part too." Up close I see that his cheeks, always round, are redder

than usual, almost circles of dark red on his brown skin. He has gold braid on his sleeves and collar, and two gold bars on each shoulder. I point to them. "Are you an officer?"

"I don't know!" he shouts. His voice is explosive, echoing across the room. "I wasn't supposed to be here. Now who's going to get us out?"

There is no one to get us out, not for a while.

I hear it, the noise I never wanted to hear again. The skritching. "Shhh," I whisper. "They're coming. Listen."

We peer into the darkness, side by side. I don't see them yet, but it's definitely the same sound. Nails skittering across the floor. The mice. I don't want to stand here and wait for them.

"The glass cabinet," I whisper urgently. "Remember what we're doing here. We have to open the cabinet."

It's behind me, like it always is, filled with lines of soldiers dressed the same as Noah. Frozen behind glass, their faces are blank. Noah flinches when he sees them, and I guess that he's imagining himself stuck behind there too, like I did. I think he's going to say again that he shouldn't be here, but he squares his shoulders. He did say he always wanted to be part of something magical. I guess he is now.

The noise is getting louder. I glance back—and there they are. Nightmare images, like zombie mice. More than last time. Five, six . . . maybe ten, with more shadows looming behind them. The candles flicker calmly, as though nothing is happening.

"We need to open it *now*," I say. I close my eyes and start humming the call. It sounds quiet, a tiny drop of sound.

"Wait," Noah says. He holds up a bugle on a chain attached to his waist. "Maybe that's what this is for?"

It's definitely ten mice now, hunched, their noses twitching as they move toward us. There are even more behind, crowds of them. I can't look. If this doesn't work . . .

"Try it," I say, breathless.

"It's like I feel what to do," he says, with the bugle in his hands. "It's calling me." He smiles hesitantly. "I'm really here."

For a moment I feel the thrill of being here again, the pure awesomeness of the magic. Then I look over my shoulder at the mice, and fear seeps back in.

Noah stands with his feet apart, left hand on the sword

at his side—how did I not notice the sword? He looks . . . different suddenly, his face set, more certain. "Attention!" he snaps, like soldiers do in movies. Nothing happens, but I feel something, a shift in the air. He puts the bugle to his lips and blows. It's strange. When he starts, it's a tiny horn, one low sound I can barely pick out, barely louder than my humming. It's not even the call, just single notes. Gradually, the sound changes. It deepens, blares, until I realize that it's not coming only from Noah anymore. Many trumpets are playing the song together, the sound of the battle call music filling the room.

The glass vanishes, and the soldiers snap to attention as one and start pouring out. They ignore us, forming row after row, sharp swords at the ready. The mice pause, eyeing this new enemy.

Then I realize the soldiers aren't fighting. They're lined up, ready to go, but not advancing. One of the mice shuffles forward.

"They're waiting for me," Noah whispers.

"No," I say, panic rising. "You can't fight, not really."

"Advance!" he calls, but the soldiers don't move. The mice creep forward, one step, two.

Noah takes a deep, shaky breath. Then he points down to his uniform. "It's clear what my part is, right? If they're going to stop the mice, I have to lead them."

Worry clenches in my chest, sending waves of *No!* through my body. This is my quest, and because I asked him to help—because I tripped—now Noah's in danger. "Are you sure?"

He takes a step forward, sword raised, and the soldiers move too. He stops and they stop. He raises his eyebrows at me. "Like Simon Says. Sort of."

I glance toward the little room where the glass cage was. "I'll go save the Nutcracker, as fast as I can. Then he'll take over."

"I think maybe I can stay back here, and they'll do the actual fighting." He looks incredibly realistic as a toy soldier, considering I know it's just him, just Noah. He stands there for a moment, in his shiny uniform, looking at the mice and soldiers clumped before him. Then he lifts his sword high above his head. "Advance!" he calls in a voice that resonates through the room, and he blows the bugle again, the familiar call.

He's enjoying this, I think. At least just a little. And

somehow he knows what he needs to do. I wish I felt even a touch of that confidence.

Somewhere a cannon blasts, and the soldiers surge forward, yelling. I can't see Noah anymore.

I need to find the Nutcracker. I move around the now-empty cabinet, through the huge white door. I step into the small room carefully, in case the Mouse King is still there, but he isn't.

The Nutcracker isn't either.

I stand there, dumb, for too long, staring at where the glass cage was. The room holds the same things as before: the chairs lined up, the closet. But the cage is gone.

For a horrible moment I'm sure the Mouse King has killed the Nutcracker already, and it's over before it even started. But this place wouldn't be here without the Nutcracker, would it?

I don't know how the magic works, but I don't think so. The Mouse King must've moved him. Or he's holding the Nutcracker some other way, somewhere else.

There's another door, on the far side. This one is painted pale blue, the color of a robin's egg. I cross the room, tentative at first, then faster. Noah is battling behind me. I have to do this quickly. The door is shut, and I panic. I can't reach the doorknobs here unless I have a ladder. I lean against the door and it moves. It's a swinging door! I push harder, press my whole weight against the wood, and it slowly gives. I peek around the edge.

There are candles—fat candles as tall as my arm—set all around the room, on tables and desks and counters. They leave the ceiling in darkness, but they're brighter, steadier than the small candles in the big room.

I'm below all the tables, doll-size, but I can see most of the room.

It's nothing like the others. They were almost completely empty, decorated with fancy furniture, more like stage settings than real rooms. This place is large, rectangular, and stuffed with simple furniture: plain wood tables, cabinets, and one dark wood rolltop desk. Every surface is covered with things. There are metal tools I don't recognize. Blocks of wood. Piles of metal springs and screws. Small cans and tubes of paint, and brushes. On the biggest table in the corner is a pile of arms and legs, waiting to be assembled. Now that I look closely, I see there are pieces of dolls everywhere: wooden hands, feet, heads, all my size. Everything is coated in a fine layer of dust.

"Drosselmeyer was a toymaker," I whisper. This must be his workshop, where he made the Nutcracker and the Mouse King.

Who would make the Mouse King on purpose?

I creep inside. There's a roar of voices from behind me, the faint sound of trumpets and violins, but it cuts off when the heavy door swings shut. I have to hurry.

"Nutcracker?" I call. But I don't even know if he can hear me in his glass box.

This place is the source of the spicy smell. The scent is thick as I move through the room, clouds of it. It smells like Christmas, or baking. I move around a table leg, peering to see. Then I stop before I trip on something.

It's the box, a man-size version of the box I have with me right now back at football practice. It's laid out flat in the middle of the floor. The lid is shut, the same swirls of words carved into the lid, each letter the size of my fist.

He's got to be shut in there. At least I know what to do now. I feel my own certainty prick through, a kind of strength inside, a calm. All I have to do is open the box.

# 19

I scramble up onto a bench and wedge my fingers under the edge of the lid, trying to pull up, but I can't budge it. It's difficult to open even the small Nutcracker box, and this lid is bigger than I am. I try again and again, then bang my hand against it in frustration. I have to get in. He's right here.

I look around for a tool, anything. Finally I see a file lying on top of a table, almost hidden under a painted wooden doll leg. I run and stand on a stool and reach for the file. I lift it, barely—it's iron, and ridiculously heavy. Though it would be a small file for a normal-size person, it's huge for me. I can't drop it. I *won't*. I drag it down, onto the stool and then the floor, panting with effort. Then I climb up onto the bench again. I slide the end of

145

the file under the edge of the lid and shove down, as hard as I can.

It moves a little. Thank God. I push again—a little more. I have an idea. I drop off the bench, keeping my hands tight on the file, and hang from it with all my weight.

The lid pops and I fall, heavy, to the ground, the file clanging on the floor next to me.

Almost there. I climb back onto the bench, push at the loose edge of the lid. It takes a lot of force, but finally it slides off, and I can see inside the box.

The Nutcracker is there, lying on his back, his eyes open and mouth grinning, but still motionless. And still sealed in that glass cage. The room is silent, my panting loud in my ears.

I want to cry. I can't even try to break the glass with my shoe—I'm wearing slippers. They're not going to break anything. I could sing part of the Nutcracker theme, I suppose. I don't know which part. Maybe the Nutcracker dance that Clara does.

I have no idea if it will work, but I can try.

I lay my hand flat on the glass and try to remember

the tune. My hand falls through, straight through, and lands on the Nutcracker's warm, real chest. The glass melted at my touch!

Noah had to break the soldiers' glass with the trumpet, and I had to break the Nutcracker's.

I pull my hand back fast, and he sits up. His eyes, so familiar, stare at me.

"You did it," he says in the rich voice I remember. "You succeeded in the first step and saved me."

"The . . . first step?" I say softly. I thought I was done here. That we were done, after tonight.

The Nutcracker climbs stiffly out of the box and bows to me. "Yes, m'lady. I have not made it past the Mouse King yet. Once we vanquish him, I will transform. And then we—all my people—can go to my home again."

I sit back on my heels. "Does . . . this happen every year?" I try to imagine one Clara each year going through this, succeeding, then hiding it. I try to imagine Ally doing it and never talking about it to anyone. I can't picture it.

He shakes his head slowly. "All the years since the first, the ballet adventure has been enough, has been all. The first performance onstage, we echo here what happens there. I almost reach my home. Then I am taken back again, to the beginning, and lie dormant until the next year, the next first performance. Sometimes, rarely, a Clara comes here and glimpses us as we truly are. A special Clara."

He stops and sighs. When he continues, his voice sounds weary and sad.

"It is two hundred years since the maker created us. He said at the beginning that the magic would last two hundred years. . . . This is the final year. It is different. We awoke early, as soon as you touched me, and began the battle. I believe that the victor, I or the Mouse King, and his people will be the only ones to survive the first performance. All else will vanish as if it never was."

I look around at the workshop. "All of this? All the soldiers . . . will vanish if you lose?"

"As if it never was," he repeats, his voice heavy.

"What about the Sugar Plum Fairy?" I ask. "Can't she help?"

"She is not here now. None of the candies are here. Just the toys and the mice. And their king."

I think of the Mouse King winning and then living ever after in this place.

Mice. Noah.

"My friend . . . he's leading your soldiers in battle against the mice. He's not really a soldier. He came here accidentally. He needs your help *now*."

"Of course." He puts one hand on his chest, like he's making a vow. "You have come to help in this great battle because you are a believer, and a Clara. A special Clara. And your friend . . . he is also a believer. There is a connection to him also, now that he has come here. With both of you together, we have a chance." He tilts his head down to me. "I will take over this battle from here. The Mouse King is hiding, I think. Watching. I must find him." He studies me for a long second. *"One battle ended. Two links forged. Those who are lost shall be found. Remember. Thank you, Clara. I will see you again soon, for the next part."*

He reaches out and touches my cheek. "What are you *doing*?"

I blink, confused. The Nutcracker didn't say that. That sounded like . . . Joey.

I rock as the floor shudders, and I'm back in the shed under the bleachers.

"Earth to Georgie. What are you doing in here?"

I open my eyes to see Joey standing in a stream of yellow light, the shed door wide open behind her.

We're back. It's still really dark in here—the light doesn't reach that far in—so I don't think she can see the Nutcracker in my arms. I tuck him under my shirt.

"Noah?" I whisper, my voice wobbling.

"Yeah. Here." As my eyes adjust, I see the familiar shape of him, blinking, standing across from me. He rubs his hands over his face, hard.

"Are you okay?" Still a whisper.

"I think so," he says, but his words sound odd, flat. "Yeah, I guess. You?"

I nod, then say yes, because he probably can't see me well either.

"I don't know if I can do that again," he says, his voice still low.

"I know this isn't a science project," Joey says. "I'm not dumb."

"We'll talk outside," I answer. "I promise. Go ahead." I need her to leave first so I can put the Nutcracker away. If she sees him, I'm toast. There's no way she'd hide that secret.

She folds her arms but doesn't leave. I can't move either. I'm still holding tight to him under my shirt. I look to Noah for help.

He sighs, takes her by the arm, and escorts her out. "Come on, let's go."

I slide the Nutcracker into the box, seal it, then put it inside my bag and zip it up. I come out of the shed only a few seconds later. Whew.

"Get off me!" Joey says, shaking Noah's hand off her arm.

"Don't be rude," I snap.

"Don't be *rude*?" she gasps. Her eyes narrow. "Are you kidding? I come to look for you and I find you under the stairs, in this shed, alone with a boy? You are in so much trouble. What were you doing, kissing?"

"No!" I say, horrified that's what she would think. That's what everyone would think. "With Noah? I would never—"

Noah throws me a dark look—like I said something awful—and shakes his head. "You can handle this yourself. Bye, Georgie."

He strides off, stomping up the stairs. I didn't even get

to tell him what the Nutcracker said, or find out what happened with him while I was gone. I wrap my hand around my bag, feeling the Nutcracker box inside. My eyes tear up.

I swallow hard and turn to Joey. "Don't tell Mom and Dad, okay?"

She snorts. "Oh, it's way too late for that. Dad sent me to look for you. Practice is over." She sniffs. "You're in for it now."

One of the assistants comes past with a string bag of balls. He gives us an odd look, then goes straight into the open shed.

Joey skips out onto the field, and I follow, biting my lip. I don't know what I'm going to say, what reason I could possibly give for leaving practice—leaving Joey alone—and going down to the shed with Noah. But I'd better think of something fast.

## 20

**M**om and Dad seem to believe that I wasn't kissing Noah—I say we were doing a science project about perception in darkness. But Joey blabs about me talking to Noah at practices, so they know I wasn't coming just because I wanted to see football or be with Dad. That counts as lying, Mom says. It's bad that I left Joey too, but the worst part is that I tried to hide what we were doing, and I went in the shed with Noah by myself.

They've never been this mad.

Dad forbids me from going to any more practices, which backfires on Joey because now she can't go either. I'm grounded except for ballet class and rehearsals. At least they still let me do those.

Noah wouldn't talk to me at school. I sat by him, of

course, and tried to ask him about what happened, but he just kept his head in his book the whole time and ignored me. I don't understand it. Kaitlyn sat stony-faced across the room, watching.

I don't even get to go to Dad's football game on Friday night, because Mom and Dad don't trust me. After class I go home and just sit in my room, pet Ginger, and stare at the ceiling.

I hate this. Somehow I messed up with everyone. Maybe I should disappear into Clara, be her instead of Georgie, and it would be easier.

The only bright spot is that we did save the Nutcracker. At least "the first step." I guess anything else that happens I'll have to do on my own.

On Saturday, I make it to the studio before everyone else, early enough to sneak the Nutcracker in. I know I can't get into the office, but if I leave him in the rehearsal room, maybe Mrs. Cavanaugh will think it's just some sort of mix-up. She and Veronica will each think the other one brought him out.

Maybe. At least they won't have any way to link me to it.

Someone's in the office with the door closed—I can see

the light—but everything else is quiet. I creep to the rehearsal studio and peer in, my bag with the Nutcracker heavy on my shoulder. The room is empty, dark. I tiptoe across the floor and jump when I see my own reflection in the big mirrors.

They always put the Nutcracker on top of the big black piano. I check over my shoulder—no one—and then set my bag on the floor and unzip it carefully. I can hardly see in the dim light from the stereo. I lift the box up and gently set it on the piano.

The lights snap on, blinding me, and I spin. Mrs. Cavanaugh stands in the doorway, one hand still on the light switch, staring at me.

I stare back, lost. I don't think I can move.

"Georgie?" she asks softly. "What are you doing?"

I want to look at the box behind me so badly, but I don't. I hold myself still like I'm in an audition. What can I say? Why would I possibly be here?

I point at my bag, open on the floor. "I . . . uh . . . forgot my bag in here last night. I just came in to get it."

She takes two steps into the room. "And no one noticed it? How . . . very strange. And you didn't even turn the lights on." Her eyes flick to the box behind me, and I hold my breath. Here it is. She knows why I'm here. She's going to kick me out of everything. She clears her throat, and I think she's getting ready to yell again. "I see. Well then," she says, quiet, dangerous. "Hadn't you better take your bag and go get ready?"

I let out all my breath. Before she can change her mind, I nod, grab my bag, and scurry to the dressing room.

She knows something. But she didn't say it. She let it go. I pull on my tights and leotard, my hands shaking, and go sit in the lobby until it's time for rehearsal, staring unseeing at the walls. Even if the Nutcracker is safe, everything else feels so broken. What happens now?

**When Mom picks me up** that night, Joey and Pip aren't with her. She called our babysitter Lisa so the two of us could have some time to ourselves.

Girls' night, she says with a smile. It's a little funny because before Will, almost everything was girls' night, and Will's with us now. He's too little and fussy—she can hardly ever leave him with someone else, even Lisa, for long. But I know what Mom means. A just-us night. That hasn't happened in a long time.

But I know she's still mad about what happened at practice, so maybe she wants to talk more about that.

We slide into a booth in our favorite Chinese restaurant, with Will gurgling in his car seat on the bench. She gets out his bottle and holds it up for him, and then she focuses on me. "So. You're not talking to Kaitlyn again. And there's this Noah. Do you want to tell me what happened?"

At first I don't tell her much. It feels like I've forgotten how to talk to her for real, especially after this week. But I try, because she's trying. I fidget and stumble on words, and she has to ask me questions. But eventually I tell her. Everything except the Nutcracker parts.

I talk about the awkwardness with Kaitlyn, the fight about lying to each other. Even about Noah. I tell her how he seems to be mad at me too. But mostly Kaitlyn. How terrible it is to feel so alone, so betrayed, after being friends for so long.

She listens to all of it. When I'm done, she sighs and tucks her dark hair behind her ear. "Sometimes," she says carefully, "friends grow apart. Interests change, and you drift away from each other."

That gives me an ache deep in the pit of my stomach. It doesn't seem right. I don't want to drift away from Kaitlyn.

"But the best friendships hold on. They have rough times, and it's okay to be mad at each other. Even grown-ups, families, get mad at each other sometimes." She smiles, her eyes crinkling. "Like this week, right? But we still love each other. If you both want to stay friends, you have to cling together and figure out how to adapt your friendship as your lives change." She's silent for a moment, one hand on Will. "I hope you know it's okay to be friends with the boy too. Noah. We were upset about your lying, not about having another friend. There's nothing wrong with having two good friends. Or a friend who's a boy."

I make a face, remembering that last look from Noah. He was—is—hurt about what I said to Joey. How I said that I would *never* kiss him, all rude like that. Even though I didn't mean it that way.

Plus whatever happened with him in the Nutcracker world. Maybe that's what scared him off. He was the one battling the mice.

Mom reaches across the table and touches my hand. "You know I'm so proud of you, right? For Clara. You had a goal, a hard goal, and you're sticking to it. No matter what happens from here on, you got the part, and you're making it happen."

I nod. I sit there for a minute, my eyes on the orange chicken in front of me. Will starts to fuss, waving his fists around.

"Do you believe in magic?" I ask.

She starts rocking Will's seat, a gentle motion, and he settles down. "Like Santa? Of course. You know that."

"No. Not like Santa." I think how to say it. "Like . . . real magic. Magic that can make real things happen." She frowns, and I can tell she doesn't understand. "Like in *The Nutcracker,* you know, how Drosselmeyer shrinks Clara and makes the soldiers come to life and everything. Could something like that really happen? Could there be something magical that could make someone . . ." I don't want to say it—it's too close to the truth—but I press on. ". . . go somewhere else? Take you somewhere else?"

The waitress interrupts to check on us, and I'm afraid Mom's not going to answer. But after she's gone, Mom's still frowning. Considering.

"Like in stories, you're thinking, right?" she starts. "I

think magic is not usually as obvious as that. We don't have it handed to us that clearly. But yes, I absolutely believe there is magic at work in the world. Every day, in big ways and small ways." She shrugs and picks up her fork. "Babies are magic. Dance is magic. Football is magic, in its own way. There are all kinds of magic." She scoops up some rice but doesn't eat it yet, holding her fork suspended in the air. "Does that answer your question?"

I don't know. Maybe. Though I've seen obvious magic too, right there in front of me. And I want it to happen again. "I think so."

"Georgie," she starts, then stops. "I don't know how to say this. But about Grandpa Reynolds . . ."

Instantly, my eyes are full. "He's not going to get better, is he?"

She studies me, serious. "Maybe not. It's hard to face. I know you love him. But he's kind of . . . stuck where he is right now. He's not getting better or worse; he's just on hold. He might have brain activity, but we can't tell. His body isn't responding anymore."

Like being locked in a glass cage, unable to move.

Oh my goodness.

"Can I visit him?" I ask. "Please? I really need to."

It's dumb—I know it is. But I broke through the Nut-cracker's glass case just by touching it, by being there. What if I could do the same for Grandpa? What if the magic carried over from the other world and I could wake him up by touching him?

She nods slowly. "Dad and I were talking about that again. They allow visitors over twelve in certain cases, with a parent. So not Joey or Pippa, but you. Dad and I think you could use a visit. If you're up for it, we thought you could go tomorrow."

"Yes," I say fervently. "I want to. As soon as I can."

She smiles and lays her hand on top of mine. We have a good, comfortable dinner, just us. We don't talk any more about this week, or even serious things. We laugh a lot. I feel better, lighter. Maybe there's a deeper purpose to all of this after all, even more than saving the Nutcracker. Maybe it's also for Grandpa, for my family.

I don't feel entirely alone anymore.

# 21

**Dad takes me** to the hospital the next day, just me and him. We're silent on the way over, listening to Dad's music, the truck bouncing on the road. I grip the armrest hard, hoping I can handle this. I've been wishing and wishing to be able to see Grandpa, but now it's kind of scary.

I've never been in a hospital before. On TV shows there are always people running around yelling, and it's crammed with sick people everywhere. This hospital is actually very neat, everything labeled and tiled and clean. It smells intensely like lemon cleaner. We take the elevator up to the fifteenth floor, Dad's arm around my shoulders. The hallway to Grandpa's room has a blue wave tiled on

the white wall, rising up and down like the water is following us . . . or leading us.

Grandma Reynolds is there when we come in, reading a book in a puffy chair under a window. She rises, so I look at her first, and she gives me a hug. She nudges her glasses up on her face and sad-smiles at Dad. "Good to see you here, Georgie. You okay?"

I nod numbly.

She brushes the hair out of my eyes. "Sweet girl. He'll be glad you came by. I think I'll go get a bite to eat. I'll be back in a while, okay?" She and Dad move to the door together, talking in low voices.

I turn my head and finally look at Grandpa.

I have to force my feet to stay there, to not run from the room.

He doesn't look like himself at all. He looks smaller, gray, his skin wrinkled and thin. There are so many wires and hoses hooked up to him that it's hard to believe he's alive under there. But I see his chest rise and fall, the monitor beeping for his heart.

I remember the birthday after we saw *The Nutcracker,*

when he presented me with the gift of lessons at a dance studio. He winked and said, "Go do it." I remember how he would always win at board games, then tell me I just have to work harder and someday I'll beat him. How he used to tell me stories when we'd sleep over there, me curled up in his big chair with him until I fell asleep. How he does that with Pippa sometimes.

How he *was* doing that with Pippa, and he can't anymore. Tears spring up. I remember the first time I saw *him* get teary, last year in the lobby after I danced in the spring show. He hugged me and told me how proud he was.

He doesn't even know I'm going to be Clara.

"It's okay," Dad says, low. I didn't hear him come in. He slips his arm over my shoulders again, and suddenly I want terribly to cry full out. A tear drips down my cheek before I can stop it. "It's scary, I know. But he's still there. I believe that. You can go and talk to him if you'd like."

I wipe my face, staring at this small, silent Grandpa, and move forward, one foot at a time.

"Do you want me to stay?" Dad asks. "Or leave you alone for a while?"

I sit gingerly on the plastic chair next to the bed. It's cold. "Alone, I think."

"Got it. I'll be back in a few. I'm right out in the hall if you need me." He disappears, and it feels different again. Like Grandpa is there, almost, right beneath the surface. In a glass cage of his own. If I can just . . .

I reach out and touch his hand, half expecting him to open his eyes and sit up, like the Nutcracker did. Be whole again, well, through the magic. I hold my breath, waiting, watching his face.

He doesn't move.

I wait, willing something to happen. But the machines keep beeping, and his chest keeps rising and falling, just the same.

I sigh. Mom said magic isn't like that. I guess it doesn't always work that way.

"Hey, Grandpa," I whisper. "It's Georgie." I squeeze his hand. "Guess what? I don't know if anyone told you, but I got Clara. I'm going to be Clara in *The Nutcracker*. Just like you said I could."

He still doesn't move, doesn't change. Nothing changes. But I imagine him smiling.

I tell him all about it, the show, and even about Noah and the real Nutcracker and Kaitlyn. Everything I've been keeping inside, that I've been too afraid to tell anyone else. When Dad comes back with Grandma, I'm telling Grandpa how I'm trying to focus on dancing as well as I can in spite of everything else.

"Can we come next week?" I ask. Dad nods, and I hug Grandpa goodbye somehow, with all the wires and everything. Then I hug Grandma too, which is easier.

Dad and I go out to lunch afterward, and we don't talk about anything much at all. I don't need to, though, because I told it all to Grandpa.

Even though it was scary and awful to see him like that, somehow I feel so much better.

**That night, after telling** everything to Grandpa, I grab the laptop and take it to my room to do some research on *The Nutcracker* and Clara.

Considering how involved I am in *The Nutcracker*, I don't know nearly enough about it. I got the book by E. T. A. Hoffmann for Christmas last year, so I know that in the original story the girl's name wasn't Clara at all—it was Marie Stahlbaum. It's still Marie in some *Nutcracker* productions, but most of the time in the ballet it's been changed to Clara.

There are a lot of different adventures in the original story, including a story within a story of Princess Pirlipat, who was cursed until the Nutcracker—really Drosselmeyer's nephew—broke it, taking over the curse himself and becoming a toy. At the end of the book, she declares that she loves the Nutcracker in spite of what he looks like, and the curse is broken. Marie/Clara marries the Nutcracker.

I look up the book first. It was published . . . yes, about two hundred years ago. The Nutcracker said it had been two hundred years since "the maker created us." But I think he meant Drosselmeyer, not E. T. A. Hoffmann.

If there is a real curse and a magical world that actually exists—including that workshop—does that mean Drosselmeyer was a real person, a proper magician, and Hoffmann wrote down the story of something true that happened? Or parts of it were true?

I search for "Drosselmeyer real." I wade through a bunch of strange links but don't find anything useful until

I see a name: Heinrich Wilhelm Drosselmeyer, born 1862, Königsberg, Prussia.

It's a genealogy site, with family members laid out in trees, like we did in first grade. I follow the branches back to the oldest person recorded: Frederick Bernhardt Drosselmeyer, born in 1792. Son of Bernhardt Drosselmeyer and Rose Marie Stahlbaum, married in 1788 in Königsberg. That's where the tree ends.

They're real. Rose Marie, the actual Clara, married a Drosselmeyer.

"Got you," I say.

"Got who?" Joey says in my ear, scaring my fingers off the keys. "What are you doing?"

I didn't hear her sneak in. "Research," I say, my jaw clenched. "For school."

She eyes me, her hair hanging, stringy, over one side of her face. "On Sunday?"

"Yes. Homework." I don't say more, don't argue with her. I've been trying not to.

Anyway, the words on the screen take over all thought. When Joey scared me, I accidentally clicked on the last link on the genealogy tree, through all the Drosselmeyers' descendants, to the very ending, the most recent people. Live people, so there are just names and no dates.

Important names. Rose Drosselmeyer married William Cavanaugh and had a daughter, Veronica.

Mrs. Cavanaugh's birth name is Rose Drosselmeyer.

Not only is the story in the ballet real, but she's related to them, to the real people, straight down the line. That's why she has the enchanted Nutcracker. They must have kept it safe all these years.

I wonder what she knows about the magic, if she knows he's still stuck in a version of that house, fighting the mice over and over. Maybe that's why she looks at me so strangely.

Maybe that's why the office door was open, even though it never had been before, right when she sent me out to the lobby by myself.

Oh, I hope she knows.

I can't talk to her, of course. But I have to tell someone else about this, how it all connects. Someone who knows about the Nutcracker and his world.

I have to find a way to talk to Noah tomorrow, even if he's mad at me.

## 22

**T**he next day, I see Noah at lunch. It looks like he's having fun, laughing with a big table of band kids. I wish I were there instead of sitting with girls I barely know. It's time to fix this.

In reading class, I sit next to him.

"Hey," I say softly.

Noah looks up. His expression has layers: surprise, hurt, dismissal. He's still angry.

He turns back to his bag, rummages for his book, and holds it up in front of his face. I take out my own book, but I don't read it yet. I place it on the desk, exactly straight, my fingers spread across the back cover.

"I'm sorry," I say, softer still. "I did really appreciate

your help, even if it didn't sound that way. What happened with you?"

He doesn't respond for a minute. Then, slowly, he lowers his book.

"I had to fight one off with a *sword*," he says, his voice flat like before.

I stay quiet, listening.

He sets the book down, leans toward me, and whispers. "I was so excited to finally be part of it. *You* know. I was doing fine, staying out of the way. But then one of the mice charged through and knocked me over, and I was on my back on that floor, and the mouse was coming down at me. He almost killed me, for real. I was looking up into his face, his sword . . . then I was in the shed."

I want to reach out and touch him, comfort the fear out of his voice, but my hands won't move. "That's horrible."

He nods and thrusts his hand through his hair, looking at the desk.

"I'm sorry," I say again.

The class bell rings, and Mr. Anderson starts talking

to the kids in the first two rows, in a low, soothing voice that almost reminds me of the Nutcracker. I wait, rubbing one finger over the slick cover of the book, but I realize Noah probably isn't going to say anything else.

"I didn't mean it," I say. "That I would never . . ." I stop. "Well. I didn't mean it."

He studies me carefully. Judging, I think, whether I'm being honest. Whether it means anything. "Yeah?"

I lean a little closer. "I really didn't mean to be rude. I was just . . . rattled. Can we be friends again? You don't have to . . . you know."

"Partake in magical adventures?" he whispers.

I laugh, loud, and Mr. Anderson's head jerks up. "Sorry," I say to him, squashing the bubbles of laughter down.

"Reading time, please," he says. "Not talking time."

Noah and I retreat into our books. After a few minutes there's a rustle, and a folded square of paper lands on my desk. I unfold it carefully. In a neat scrawl, it says:

I choose to partake in the magical adventures.
Talk later?

I grin at him over my book. Yes, we can talk later. I can tell him about Mrs. Cavanaugh, how everything is linked. That wasn't as hard as I was afraid it would be. And it was the right thing to do, no matter what happens next.

**Even though Noah and I** are ready, nothing happens for more than a month. I can't get to the Nutcracker's world. I keep waiting, every time I pick him up and dance with him, for something to happen, for the next part to begin. I wonder what "soon" means in his time. It's the end of November. We have only a couple of weeks of rehearsal left before it's time for the first performance . . . and the Nutcracker's deadline.

Has he been fighting the mice this whole time? Hunting the Mouse King? Returned to the glass box? There's no way for me to know.

It's not until a Sunday, in Clara rehearsal, that things finally start to happen again.

It's me, Ally, the Fritzes, and Peter. Mrs. Cavanaugh has us go through all the Clara parts from the very beginning, running them together for the first time. We do the opening dance, then mark our parts in the party scene until Drosselmeyer and Peter arrive. Mrs. Cavanaugh plays Drosselmeyer again, stalking into the party. We go to the section where she hands me the Nutcracker, and I nearly drop him when I take him in my arms. He's warm again.

I run back to my place, my nerves jangling. "Hi, Nutcracker," I whisper so no one else can hear me.

Will I go? Is this the time?

Before the music even starts, I'm there. But not in the big room. I'm somewhere else, in a pink-and-blue room with toys everywhere. Like the big room, it has a wood floor, but this one is made of pale slats, with round yellow and blue rugs like lakes of pastel color, though darkened by the candlelight. All around the room are dolls and toy animals, my size or bigger, with a huge rocking horse that could crush me if I moved too close to it. All the furniture—a bed, a plush chair, a dresser—are bright white. The room is quiet, still. Something smells too sweet, like burnt vanilla.

I look around quickly for what might have brought me here. Nothing moves. Is there anything from the ballet? I scan the neat rows of toys propped on the shelves for anything I recognize, anything that looks out of place. I know I don't have much time.

I see a bugle that looks like the one Noah used, hanging on a hook. I touch it gently. It's slightly warm, but nothing happens.

*There.* There's one toy that's locked in a glass case of its own, propped up in the far corner. A bear, wild and fierce, its claws raised. Bigger, wider than me. It stands almost to the ceiling. Its teeth are bared, snarling at air.

"Hello?" I step forward. "Are you the one I'm supposed to help?"

He can't reply, but I know the answer. In the ballet, Drosselmeyer brings a bear to the party scene to dance for the guests. If this bear is behind glass, he must be on the Nutcracker's side.

I can't waste time. I run to the case, thrust my hands against the glass, and feel it melt beneath my palms like mist.

The bear comes alive and steps out, roaring ferociously. I shrink back from him and crouch in a ball on the blue rug. He comes closer, his roar splitting my ears.

Maybe it was a mistake, and I wasn't meant to release him after all. . . .

Suddenly I'm back in the studio, at the end of the Clara dance, my pulse hammering. Sweat drips down my back. I get the old surprised, pleased look from Mrs. Cavanaugh. She even winks at me.

That's all that happens during rehearsal, even though I dance with the Nutcracker several times. But it's started again, and I have to be ready at any time.

After rehearsal, Peter pulls me aside in the hall and waits, one hand on my arm, until the others go past. I still haven't really talked much to him, not alone at all. Ally is always there. "Is everything okay?" I ask.

He shrugs, a huge shrug. "Yes. It is fine with me." His accent is thick. He's a little hard to understand, but fun to listen to. "I want to say . . . I watch you dance, you know. Sometimes you are different. Your dancing transforms you." He looks down at me over his nose, his eyes distant, face serious. "This place, this piece, it is *magiya*, yes? It is perhaps . . . *sudba*."

"*Magiya?*" I repeat. "Does that mean 'magic'?"

He looks surprised. "Yes. Do you not see it?" He shrugs

again, spreads his arms wide. "I am surprised not everyone see it. It is right there, in the room with us."

I smile slowly. "I do see it."

He nods. "I thought. You do well. You are good dancer. Do not worry so, yes?" We walk together to the lobby. Then he squeezes my shoulder and breaks away to head upstairs alone.

I wonder for a moment if he goes to that world too. But he doesn't ever touch the Nutcracker. Besides, I don't think that's what he was saying. I think he was just telling me he *sees* the magic, sees somehow that I'm wrapped up in it. But what was that other word he said . . . *sudba*? It's magic and maybe *sudba*?

I borrow one of the older dancer's phones and look up the word on the Internet. Russian, *sudba*.

It comes right up. It's not spelled like that at all in Russian. It starts with *cy,* and it has other weird letters.

But it means . . . 'fate.'

That night I call Noah and tell him everything that happened. He goes quiet when I tell him about the bugle. Suspiciously quiet.

"What?" I ask.

He clears his throat. I can hear someone laughing in the background. "I think I saw . . . well. I'd better go look first. I'll tell you if it's anything."

He hangs up, and I flop back on the floor. I wish he'd tell me *now*.

# 23

**The next day** I decide that now that things are good with Noah, I want to see what I can do about Kaitlyn. I think about what Mom said, how if you want to stay friends, you have to cling together. I want to be friends with her again. It's been way too long.

I ask Mom to get us to school early, and even though Joey complains, we make it. I park myself outside near the front steps so I'll see everyone who comes. It's cold in that frosty November way, the grass sharp under my feet, the wind trying to find cracks in my coat. I shiver and stuff my hands in my pockets, but I don't go inside. Kids start to arrive, at first trickling from cars in twos and threes. I watch the line of cars from across the lawn, more lining up every second. Then a bus pulls up, and another, and a great mass of kids surges through. I stand there until I see Kaitlyn come, on the third bus, and trudge up the path.

I step into her way. "Hey. Can we talk?"

She sighs. "I thought we did this." She walks with me anyway. Her hair's different than I've ever seen it, in a dark braid curling all the way around her head, and I want to say something about it, but I don't. It would be strange to start that way.

At first I don't say anything. Even though I planned out what I wanted to say, it's different in real life when she's right in front of me. My tongue freezes.

"Congratulations," she says as we go through the doors.

I frown. "On what?"

"On being Noah Waterston's girlfriend. You two are cute together." The words come out bitter, the opposite of what they say.

"I'm not . . ." I shake my head. "That's not what I want to talk about." We have to separate around some slow people, then come back together. It's almost too warm in the hallway, after I've been standing outside for so long. My cheeks feel hot. "I am friends with Noah.

Good friends. But that doesn't mean I can't be friends with you too."

"Doesn't it?" She stops and faces me, and now we're the ones people push around. We're standing almost in our normal meeting spot. "Isn't that why we're not friends anymore?" I hate the expression on her face, the hardness. Hate more that it's for me. "You lied to me so you could hang out with him instead."

"*No*. I really didn't, not ever." I take a deep breath. "The truth is, there was—*is*—something going on that Noah has been helping me with. With *The Nutcracker*. And I couldn't tell you because . . . of Clara. I didn't think I could at least, that it would be too awkward. But I want to now. It's big, Kait. Will you come and eat lunch with me and Noah, and we can tell you about it?"

Her eyebrows are raised high, and I can see the curiosity, the old Kaitlyn who was my best friend. Then they snap down, and all I see is anger.

"No," she says. "Bye, Georgie." She shoves past me into the crowd.

I stand there alone, lost, until the bell rings and I have to go to class.

• • •

**At party scene rehearsal** that night, all the women and girls, me included, wear big fake rehearsal hoop skirts so we can get used to moving in them. They're basically skirts made of circles of wire covered in linen fabric. They're ingenious—the circles get bigger as they go down, so the hoop makes any skirt worn over it full, but they collapse flat when you take the hoop off. Ours go just to our knees, but the ones the mothers wear go from their waists all the way down to their feet, like bells. When they wear the real costume dresses in performances, you can't even see their feet. They look like they're gliding across the stage.

Tonight they're a bit awkward, their skirts smashing down when they get too close to each other. It's strange having the extra weight of the hoop around my waist, and I learned last year that it forces you to stand, most of the time. You can kneel on the floor, but if you sit, or even lean against something, the hoop poufs up in front of you and shows the pantaloons underneath.

Still, after a while I get tired waiting for Mrs. Cavanaugh to work out an issue with the music, and I forget and sit on the floor.

 182

The front of the hoop flies up and smacks me in the face.

There's a laugh above me, and I scramble to my feet. It's Ally. Of course. But her laugh doesn't actually sound mean this time, just amused. She meets my eyes and shrugs.

"These things are a pain, am I right?" She leans next to me against the wall and watches the others.

She's never willingly hung out with me before. Or said anything remotely nice. Huh.

I smooth down the skirt and wonder what it would have been like to be the real Clara and have to wear one all the time during the day. Definitely a pain.

Then it's second cast's turn, and we start from the beginning of the party scene. Most of the time we get much further now before someone messes up, before Mrs. Cavanaugh stops us. She takes notes and then tells us afterward if the mistakes aren't too bad.

Even though I want to help the Nutcracker, I'm glad I don't go away every time I hold him anymore. I like doing the dances myself.

I get him from Drosselmeyer, who winks at me, and I take the Nutcracker around to show him off. Even though he's not warm, or "alive," I still feel like he's mine. I do the dance—step, step, hop, chassé, turn—and Mrs. Cavanaugh doesn't stop me. I run forward, hold him up high, and Justin takes him. Runs with him across the room, pretends to slam him down . . .

And drops him. I hear the crack even over the music. I think everyone does. Mrs. Cavanaugh's face drains to paper white. Every person in the room turns to Justin, staring in horror at his feet.

Mrs. Cavanaugh is the first one there, and I'm the second. "Is he okay?" I whisper.

She doesn't answer me. She leans over him, an echo of Drosselmeyer when he fixes the Nutcracker in the ballet. She picks him up reverently, muttering something under her breath. For a shocked moment I imagine it's a spell, and she's a witch, before I realize she's cursing.

His left arm is snapped off at the shoulder.

I don't even think of the doll in front of me—I think of the real Nutcracker. "How can he fight without his arm?" I say, my voice soft.

Mrs. Cavanaugh's head shoots up, and she stares at me hard. I hold her gaze, willing her to know what I mean, that I'm helping him. That I know he's from her family and that he's real.

"That's all for today," she shouts to the whole room. "I'll see you all next time."

She cradles the Nutcracker, his broken arm tucked in next to him. She looks at me once more, then whisks out the door.

The rest of us stand uncomfortably silent. Justin bursts into noisy tears and runs out, probably looking for his mother. That somehow frees everyone else to move, to take off the hoops, and to head, whispering, for the door.

I untie my hoop too and drop it on the pile of collapsed rings. Then I run down the hall, past the gossiping people. I hear someone wondering aloud why it's such a big deal, that yes, it's old, but it's just a prop.

I know better. I have to see for myself if he's all right, if Mrs. Cavanaugh can fix him before the battle. Maybe I can tell her I'll help. Maybe she'll know why. But when I get to the lobby, she's shut in the office, the door a blank, harsh barrier. I don't dare knock.

But no one will be here to pick me up for forty minutes. So I curl up on the bench, my knees pulled to my chest, and watch the people who drift around me, packing up, driving away. I stare at the closed door. I wonder if Mrs. Cavanaugh—if the Nutcracker—can feel my worry pulsing through it.

She hasn't come out by the time Mom finally comes and I have to run upstairs and change in a rush.

Mrs. Cavanaugh has to be able to fix him, make him able to fight. Otherwise the Mouse King is going to win.

# 24

**T**he next morning, I wait for Noah before school, instead of Kaitlyn. His reaction is so different. His whole face lights up, and we fall right into step together.

"Did something happen last night?"

I swallow hard, tears pricking behind my eyes again. "He's broken. The Nutcracker . . . Justin dropped him, and his arm snapped off."

Noah frowns. "Can they fix him?" We pass a group of band kids in the hall, and he waves, half smiles, and turns back to me. "Glue or something?"

I shrug. "Maybe. I don't know. But right now he's locked up in the office, and you know she's going to be more careful with him now. How am I going to get back to help? How are *we*, if you're supposed to go back again too?"

 187

His face goes still, almost scared, and it's my turn to frown. "What? You don't want to go back? That's okay. . . ."

"It's not that." He twists his mouth sideways, like he's thinking. "I haven't tried yet . . . but do you think . . . ?" He pauses for a really long time, his eyes all distant. Finally I poke him in the shoulder, and he jumps. We stop in front of his locker. "Do you think there might be another object from that world that could take us there?" he asks.

I shake my head. "How could there be? It'd have to be like two hundred years old."

He nods slowly, and the bell rings before he can say anything else. At lunch we sit together, but he's quiet, and in reading he just stares at his book. He doesn't mention the Nutcracker again.

Not super helpful, but there's nothing I can do either. At rehearsal I ask Mrs. Cavanaugh if the Nutcracker is okay, and all she says is "Don't worry. He will be ready."

Then her face goes hollow, and she says she doesn't know if she is going to unnecessarily risk him with "this cast" anymore for regular rehearsals.

Then I won't have any chances at all.

• • •

**The next day, Noah** isn't there.

At lunch I sit by myself and keep waiting for him to come, but he doesn't. I figure he had a dentist appointment or something. Sometimes people do that at lunch. But he's not in reading either, and fear starts to bloom. I see Kaitlyn's eyes on me. I meet them once, frowning.

He said he'd be here. He never misses school, and he would've told me. After sixth period I break down and go to the office to see if anyone knows where he is. It would be on record if he called in sick.

Mrs. Kenworthy gets grim when I ask. She looks over her shoulder at the principal's closed door, then lowers her voice. "Are you friends with Noah, dear? I'll make a note. The police may want to talk to you too at some point. He's been missing since last night. They think he might have run away."

The words tangle in my head. He hasn't run away. He's gone somehow, without me. Whatever he was talking about, another object, his idea . . . he found it, and he went. Maybe the Mouse King has him, and now he's like the Nutcracker, stuck in a glass cage. And I have no way to get there.

I try to call him when I get home, but no one answers. The phone rings and rings, echoing.

Missing.

It's my fault, every second of it. And I don't think he's going to get out of it without me.

I tell Mom that Noah is missing, and her face looks like Mrs. Kenworthy's did. But she doesn't know about the Nutcracker or the Mouse King, so she says maybe the police are right, that he's run away or is hiding somewhere. I almost tell her the rest, but I don't know how, don't know if I should. Instead I go to my room, curl up under my blanket, and cry.

I try to convince Mom to let me stay home the next day, that I feel sick. Maybe I can do something, try to find Noah. Or maybe I should be home in case he comes back. She won't let me. She says it'll be better for me to have other things to think about, my normal routine.

She's wrong. I can't do anything at school, can't think of a single thing except Noah and the Nutcracker and the Mouse King. I picture Noah fighting those nightmare mice all on his own. I picture him losing. I feel an ache in my chest, heavy, constant. I don't talk to anyone. Everyone else is quiet too. It was on the news last night, that Noah is missing. There was an Amber Alert in case he was abducted.

At lunch I sit at my old, empty table, staring at the lonely space across from me. Until Kaitlyn slips into it. We study each other for a long moment, silent. Then she takes her sandwich out of the bag and places it on top, neat, like she always does.

"Tell me," she says, her face serious again. "What you were going to tell me before. What you and Noah have been doing."

I swallow hard, and then I tell her everything. Every last bit. She doesn't believe me at first—and she asks lots of questions, making me explain every detail of how it happened. How I went, what the Nutcracker said, and how Noah got involved.

By the time we're done eating, she believes me. I expect her to tell me that I need to talk to a grown-up, that I need to tell someone else all of this so they understand what's going on. We don't disappear when we go, so Noah must be somewhere in this world, somewhere they haven't looked. He just needs to be found and pulled out. But I have no idea where he would be.

I've been considering talking to a grown-up myself, all day.

"They'd never believe you," Kaitlyn says matter-of-factly. "They'd think you were crazy or you were both doing drugs or something, and it would just make them more confused. Let them keep looking for him." She glares at me. "I am mad at you for not telling me all this, Georgie. Really mad."

My chest feels even worse, a swirling mass of anxiety. "I'm sorry. I don't know why I didn't."

"I don't either." She shrugs. "Well, maybe. We were . . . not exactly in a good place, as my mom says."

Plus it's related to Clara, which would have been tough to talk about.

She frowns. "Anyway. What are you going to do now?"

I shake my head. "I don't *know*. I can't go on my own."

"Unless you're dancing with the Nutcracker. Wait." She raises an eyebrow. "You have tech rehearsal at the theater tonight, you said? Won't he be there?"

I run a finger across the lunch table, the ugly smooth plastic, thinking. "He might. Or Mrs. Cavanaugh might keep him in the office so she doesn't risk him."

"Get hold of him," she says. "As soon as you can. If he's not there, we're just going to have to find a way to break you into the studio so you can get to him." She sees my face. "What? Noah is *missing,* Georgie. You don't know what's going on over there, but it can't be good. You have to work fast."

I nod. I'm *so* glad she's with me again, on my side. I needed her.

If I broke into the studio, even if I found a way to do it, I'd probably be caught. Arrested. Kicked out of *Nutcracker* and Mrs. Cavanaugh's studio for good.

But Kaitlyn's right. Noah is in real, serious danger.

I have to do whatever it takes to get Noah out of this.

# 25

**That night is our first** rehearsal at the Wilson Theater, not far from my house. It's a huge place, with red plush seats in tiers, an orchestra pit, and a lovely big stage. Dad said *Nutcracker* is the theater's biggest moneymaker of the year, so we move in and take it over for the next month.

I know the backstage, the dressing rooms, and the green rooms well already, from the three years I've been in the show. So I know right where I should go when I get there—the massive girls' dressing room upstairs, where I was last year. We don't need to dress in costume tonight, but I need to drop off my bag, change into leotard and tights, and head to the stage for warm-ups.

I'm tempted to go straight backstage instead, but I'd be too noticeable in street clothes. I'd get sent back upstairs anyway. So I go, change as fast as possible, and run downstairs. I have to be early. I have to have time to look for the Nutcracker.

I'm lucky, and there aren't many dancers down here yet. Tech people are in the wings, working on the light boards and whatever else is there, and Mrs. Cavanaugh is onstage talking to someone. The lights are on and the barres are set up onstage, but only a few people are using them, mostly older dancers. And Ally, stretching on the floor.

I slide past the tech people and into the narrow passageway behind the back screen. I run, silent in my ballet slippers, to the other side of the stage, where the prop tables are. It's deserted on this side right now. One table is all laid out with props for Act 2: the Spanish castanets, Chinese fans, Arabian cloths. I glance over my shoulder. People could see me from the stage if they looked.

I move quickly to the second table, the downstage one. Here are the things for Act 1, the battle scene—a stack of wooden guns and swords, but not my candle. I enter from the other side on a quick change, so Mrs. Cavanaugh said the candle would stay over there. The party scene props and a pile of the practice hoop skirts are on this table too. And in the back, pushed up against the wall so it can't be knocked over, is the box.

He's here.

"What are you doing?"

I spin, my back to the table. Ally stands in the wings, arms folded. She purses her thin lips. "Well? You're skulking."

"I was . . ." My throat is suddenly dry. I turn to the table and gesture. "I was checking the props. But I don't see the candle for the beginning of the battle scene. Isn't it supposed to be here?"

The suspicion on her face is wiped away by scorn. "It's on the other *side*. Remember? She specifically told us on Monday. Do you pay attention?"

"Right. I forgot." I laugh nervously.

She sighs, and her face loosens a little. "Don't freak out so much. You'll be fine." She tilts her head toward the stage. "Come warm up. You don't want to get caught wandering over here."

I follow her to the barres under the hot lights. I already did get caught once. I can't get caught again.

**Tech rehearsals are always** long, full of stops and starts while they fix lights, marks on stage, and entrance and exit timings, all the things you can only do in the real performance space. This one is the longest I've ever been in. Mrs. Cavanaugh is doing most of the run-through with Ally and the first cast, so the rest of us have to sit in the audience seats and watch, trying to pay attention to changes, as they go on and on and on. The real Nutcracker is brought out for Ally to use, so at least there's that. I try to look at him from down in the seats. He looks whole, as far as I can tell. His arm is there.

I wish it were me holding him.

At least I get to go up for my soldier part in the battle scene, to fight with the grown-ups who are playing mice. It'd be fun if I could concentrate on it. I keep glancing at the cradle at the back of the stage, where Ally/Clara left the Nutcracker. I feel him, like he's calling to me. It's horrible, being so close but not being able to go. I keep thinking of Noah, maybe fighting the mice for real.

Finally it's over, and Mrs. Cavanaugh calls for a ten-minute break before we do second cast.

Almost. Almost. I'm coming, Noah.

**It's not until we're** already rehearsing—I'm standing there in my hoop skirt onstage, pretending to talk to the party girls—that I consider that I might not go when I dance with him. That this is a Hail Mary—one last, desperate try to win—and it might not even work.

It has to work.

I mess up and go to the wrong mark next, but I don't think Mrs. Cavanaugh notices. She doesn't stop us for that. Though a couple minutes later she adjusts the lights again, not happy with what they set with Ally, so we have to stand there and hold our positions while the techs check the reds and the blues. I'm about to pop out of my skin with impatience.

At last we start again, working our way through the party scene. We hit Drosselmeyer's music, and my heart matches the beat, sharp and strong.

Drosselmeyer presents the other gifts: the doll, who does her solo, and then the bear. I think of the real bear, the one I freed, and what he might be doing now. Then Drosselmeyer gives Fritz's present. Then, at last, mine.

I run forward to accept the Nutcracker, barely remembering the part I'm supposed to play onstage. I wrap my arms around him. He's warm. He seems okay, though his mended arm looks a little funny, out of line. I take him back to my place.

The dark wood floor stretches before me. I'm there.

# 26

I **expected a battle** in progress, chaos and smoke and trumpets. But it's quiet and still, like the first time I came. The cabinet is empty, the glass gone. I step forward, breathing in the familiar wax and pine smells. "Noah?" I call. "Where are you?"

I listen. There's pressure on my ears, and somewhere I hear a tiny drip that might be a candle. Nothing else.

"Noah?"

No reply.

"Nutcracker?" I try shouting. "Can you hear me?"

Nothing.

I don't have much time. I run for the door to the little room, but it's firmly shut, the doorknob miles above my head. I don't think I could reach it even if I had a normal-

size chair to stand on, and all I have are giant ones. I pound on the door. "Noah! Are you in there?"

I press my ear against the thick wood. I think I hear something, faint. A voice. It might be Noah's. But I have no way to get in.

Something rustles behind me. I move back into the darkness and hold my breath. Skittering. It must be a mouse.

I watch as it shuffles out of the wall near the trunk of the great tree, bolts across the room, and disappears behind the cabinet. Faint rustling again, and then it's gone.

I check for any other movement, then run across the floor to look at the spot by the tree that the mouse came from. It's well hidden in the shadows of branches, but it's there. A mousehole, bigger than me. Behind it is the dark, empty stretch of a tunnel.

"Lights!" Mrs. Cavanaugh yells. I blink in the sudden brightness at the people around me. We're at the end of the doll dance, when we all have to put the toys away. The Nutcracker is at my feet, in the cradle, bandaged by Drosselmeyer. I suck at the air, trying to readjust to here, now, but still wrapped up in what I saw.

I'm certain that Noah's stuck there, somewhere. I'm going to have to go back tonight. And I'm going to have to go into that tunnel.

Mrs. Cavanaugh calls a five-minute break before we do the battle scene, and I'm suddenly drenched with nerves again. I have to do something I've only done a couple of times before. I have to lie to Mom.

I go to the house phone in the green room, as quick as I can before anyone else comes in. I wait, tapping my foot, while the phone rings.

"Hello?" Mom answers. Will is yelling in the background, and Pip is singing.

"It's me," I say. "Mrs. Cavanaugh asked us to call. . . ." I talk fast, before I lose my nerve. "Rehearsal is running really late, and she's treating us to some pizza after. We don't know how long it's going to be . . . so Veronica said she'll bring me and Ally home."

The late part is totally believable; tech rehearsals have run as late as ten o'clock before. I don't know if Mom will believe the other part, but I wanted to make sure I'll have enough time. When I do call to have her pick me up, she'll know I lied, and it'll be bad. Mrs. Cavanaugh will be furious—she might not even let me perform. But Noah will be safe then, if all goes well. That's more important. And if all goes really well, I can save the Nutcracker too.

If it doesn't go well—I can't think about that.

Mom sighs. "On a Thursday? She realizes you're still in school, right?"

"I know. But you know how it is, this close. Especially with Clara."

Will's scream gets louder, sharper, and she sighs again. "Okay. I'll see you when I see you. Love you."

I can't answer for a second, I feel so bad. Scared, even. I almost wish I could just go home like normal. But I think of Noah's mom, probably frantic about where he is. "Love you too."

I hang up. Then I make another quick phone call, just to be safe.

Rehearsal goes on and on, stopping every few minutes through the battle scene, until I was right anyway about running late. At nine-fifteen, Mrs. Cavanaugh calls it a night, and we all scatter back to the dressing rooms.

I change, same as usual, chatting to everyone as best I can. I say goodbye and head downstairs, my dance bag thumping on my hip. But instead of going outside to wait with everyone else, I duck back into the stage area. I have to be careful—there are still techs down here, finishing up whatever they do—but I figure I can say I forgot something, if I have to. That excuse worked before.

No one notices me. I hurry back behind the screen again, over to the far side of the stage. The props are still there, laid out on the table, ready for tomorrow's rehearsal. I was afraid he wouldn't be there, that Mrs. Cavanaugh would take him home with her. But he's waiting for me.

I grab his box and duck behind the curtain and into the little hidden stairwell to the front balcony that no one ever uses, at least in this show. I don't go up, though. I just sit at the bottom of the steps and rest the box on my lap. It's pitch dark, the air heavy with dust. No one will look for me here.

When I'm sure no one's followed me, I open the box as quietly as I can. Then I pull the Nutcracker to my chest, stand, and sway. It's time to go.

# 27

**I**t **worked. The room** is the same as before, empty. I'm in my Clara nightgown and slippers.

"Noah?" I call. "Nutcracker?"

No one answers. I have to go into the mouse tunnel.

I have to not let myself imagine for even a second what it would be like to run into one of those mice while stuck in a dark tunnel, or I won't be able to go.

I run to the entrance by the tree, take a deep breath, and dive in. The darkness swallows me. It's cool and damp and smells like animals.

I wish fiercely that I had my cat, Ginger, with me. Even if she were tiny like me, she'd take the mice on. Or if she were big, bigger than them . . . but then I picture a giant

Ginger batting me with her claws and realize that might not be a good idea after all.

There's enough light from somewhere that I can just make out the tunnel curving ahead of me, the smooth walls. I walk forward as fast as I dare. Then it gets dark again and I can't see anything. I keep going, slower. Suddenly there's air on my face, and I stop and feel the wall with my hands. The tunnel branches, left and right. Like the start of a maze.

I fight the panic of getting trapped in here, lost, circling the same tunnels in darkness forever. It feels like that could happen, with this kind of magic. Or I could get stuck just long enough that I vanish too when the rest of this place does, when Ally does the first performance. My hands shake so badly that I cross them over my chest.

I choose to go to the right. When it branches again, I choose right again, hoping the path will curve back around to the house, where I need to be. I push through the darkness, forward, my thoughts fixed on Noah. He's here somewhere. I can't give up on him.

There's a noise behind me, and I freeze. No. The tunnel's not wide enough for me and a mouse. The mice will find me and attack. The noise is louder, shuffling. I press against the side anyway, my hands flat on the dirt wall, and hold my breath. The shuffling gets even louder. I close my eyes, try to make myself as small as I can. Maybe it will work. Maybe.

The sound veers off, then slowly gets quieter again. The mouse took another tunnel. I breathe in little gasps and start to run. I hurtle through the dark: straight, then curved, then straight. . . .

Suddenly there is light. Candles. A voice. I stop at the tunnel exit. It's the workshop, jumbled with all the tables and bits of toys. The giant box in the center is gone. In its place is Noah, in his bright red soldier uniform, tied to the leg of a massive chair. In front of him, pacing back and forth and muttering in a high, squeaky voice, is the Mouse King. Off in the corner I see the Nutcracker, crumpled on the ground, unmoving.

I bite back a cry. I can't worry about him yet. I have to get Noah.

"She will come," the Mouse King squeaks. "She will come to save you. I feel it. And then I will get the other, and there will be no Claras. No performance." He squeaks, a high, piercing call, and starts pacing again. "Then I will win."

I look around for something to hit him with. It's all I can do. He won't have any idea I'm here yet, that I'm coming from the tunnel. There's a low bench next to me scattered with toy pieces, but most everything is too big: arms, legs, a head that looks like Pinocchio, everything too heavy and awkward for me to lift without the Mouse King hearing.

Then I see it. A shoe. Bright blue, carved, just big and heavy enough.

I slide sideways and pick up the shoe. It's heavy in my hand, solid. I tiptoe forward, slowly, silent, keeping myself behind the Mouse King. Noah sees me, and his eyes go round. He doesn't say a word. I dart in, the shoe held high, and throw it, the way Dad taught me to throw a football. Hard, straight, accurate.

It smacks the Mouse King in the back of the head with a satisfying *thunk*. There's a pause, when nothing happens. When he could turn around and roar and charge at me.

But he doesn't turn. He slowly tips over and crashes to the ground, like a character in a cartoon. It must be the magic. All I had to do was hit him.

I leap straight for Noah and start fumbling with the rope. "Are you okay?" I ask. "Did he hurt you?"

"You did it," he says, staring at the downed Mouse King. I get a knot undone, but the rope is double-tied. I work on the second knot. "You hit him with your shoe." He twists to look at me over his shoulder and laughs. "Just like Clara's supposed to. Did you do that on purpose?"

I snort. "No. I just grabbed it. It's *sudba*."

"It's what?"

"Tell you later." I get the knot untied, and the rope drops to the floor.

I jump forward and hug him. It surprises both of us, but I can't help it. I didn't realize how worried I was until I saw him there, in real danger. He hesitates, then puts his arms around me too. "I'm glad you're okay," I whisper.

We let go and step back, quick. He tries to push his

hair up, but his hand bangs into the brim of his hat. He laughs and looks down at the floor.

"We should see if the Nutcracker's all right," he says, his voice low. "He was trying to rescue me. The Mouse King hit him hard just before you came."

We go quickly to the Nutcracker. I lean over him and gently touch his shoulder. He's alive. His breathing is soft, even, as if he's asleep. "Wake up," I say. "It's okay. I got the Mouse King. I think he's dead. It's over."

He takes a breath, ragged, then slowly moves and sits up. "Clara! And young prince, you're free." He rubs his left arm, the one Justin broke. I can tell it's stiff, awkward. "What happened?"

"I hit the Mouse King and killed him," I repeat, a little pride creeping into my voice. "With a shoe. Just like the ballet."

He shakes his head. "No."

I frown. "I did! Just now . . ."

"If he were dead, I would have transformed. You must have stunned him. We must check—beware!"

He scrambles to his feet and shoves us out of the way,

hard. We tumble in different directions, like bowling pins. I land on the floor a couple of feet away, and then I see it.

The Mouse King stands there, curved sword raised high. He would've killed us if the Nutcracker hadn't jumped in. He would've sliced us into pieces.

# 28

The Mouse King swings, aiming at the Nutcracker, but the Nutcracker dodges and draws his own sword. They circle, eyeing each other like dancers. The Mouse King squeaks again, a long, earsplitting cry. The Nutcracker's left arm hangs from his side. I don't think it works anymore.

"*Soldiers!*" the Nutcracker shouts, pointing to Noah. Noah frowns.

"The horn!" I yell. "He needs help. Blow the horn!"

Noah pulls the bugle from his side and plays the battle call. Soldiers pour into the room from both doors. Mice pour in from the holes. They immediately start fighting, mouse to soldier, yelling and squeaking. The bear is there too, slashing at mice with his claws. Even the doll is there.

212

I see her give one of the mice a massive kick and knock him over. The Nutcracker lunges forward, stabbing at the Mouse King, who fights him off and slashes back.

I don't move, sitting there, stunned, on the floor. It happened in seconds. We went from victory, safety—I thought—to this mess, soldiers and mice fighting everywhere around me, in seconds. I see a soldier hack at a mouse and blood come gushing out. Real blood. I can't take it in. It's not like the ballet battle scene, with everyone only pretending to fight. It doesn't feel like a show anymore.

My eyes meet Noah's. He's staring too, standing on the other side of the fighting Mouse King and Nutcracker. "Watch out!" he calls. "Get somewhere safe!"

*Because that's what Clara does in the battle scene,* I think numbly. She hides at the front of the stage because it's too much, because she can't look at it. Until she finally gets up and joins in by throwing her shoe. But I already did that, and the battle didn't end. A soldier screams, and I shut my eyes.

No. I can't pretend it's not happening. I'm part of this. I'm an important part of this.

I open my eyes and push myself to my feet. Noah has his sword out, though it doesn't seem as if he knows what to do with it. I look for the shoe I threw. Maybe I can find it again. Maybe I can throw it again and finish the job this time. But I don't see it anywhere. There isn't any battle smoke in here, but it feels like there is, like there should be. There should be music soaring, drums and cymbals clashing. A cannon. Except there is no music. There are screams and shrieks and grunts. Every time a sword lands, there's more blood. It's hard to breathe.

Noah helped with the battle call, and he can at least defend himself. I don't have a sword, or even a shoe. Yet I have to find some way to help.

But I don't want to kill. Even if I had a sword, I don't think I could use it. I don't like fighting. And this feels so *wrong*. It's like all my senses are jangling at once, clashing, telling me *no*.

I think of E. T. A. Hoffmann's original story. Unlike in the ballet, the Nutcracker isn't transformed when he kills the Mouse King. He does bring Marie the Mouse King's crowns, but that isn't what changes him. He's transformed when Marie says she loves him no matter what he looks like. In the book, that's what ends the curse and changes him back into a prince.

I don't think they're supposed to be fighting at all.

I know what to do.

I clench my fists. *"Stop!"* I yell as loud as I can.

The frenzy slows, and a few battles stop. But most of the mice and soldiers keep fighting. The Nutcracker and Mouse King continue to battle, intent on each other. *"Stop!"* I yell again. "Listen to me! Please!"

This time everyone stops. Even the Mouse King is rigid, his sword fixed in the air as he faces me. I look at him, this terrible, frightening creature, and remember the toys in the theater gift shop, the three-headed mice. Little kids buy them, play with them. Love them.

Who would make the Mouse King on purpose, I'd wondered. But Drosselmeyer did. And not for this.

"You're toys!" I say into the silence. "That's what this place is, a workshop. Drosselmeyer didn't create magic creatures to fight and kill. He made *toys*."

Noah lowers his sword, listening. I see one or two other soldiers lower theirs too.

"I think . . ." I see all the faces staring me down, and

I take a deep breath. "I *know* you're not supposed to fight each other. Not like this. Did Drosselmeyer?" I turn to the Nutcracker, standing as still as if he were locked in glass again. "Did he tell you to fight, when he made you real for Marie?"

The silence is so long I don't think he's going to answer. "He told us not to," he says finally. "We were supposed to have a mock battle for the crowns, but I killed it." He glances at the Mouse King. "Him. I killed him instead of pretending."

I nod. "You disobeyed Drosselmeyer by doing that. So he cursed you to keep doing it. For two hundred years."

Everyone's quiet, considering. Understanding suddenly that everything, all of this, is different than they thought.

"Lay down your swords," the Nutcracker says, gruff. Every soldier, including Noah, places his sword on the floor with a tremendous clatter. The Nutcracker does too, right in front of the Mouse King, then holds his hands high.

The Mouse King stares, his whiskers twitching, his face unreadable. Then he lays his sword down too. The mice step back.

I stopped them. I can't quite believe it worked. They listened to me.

"I think that's why you needed a real Clara this time. A real person," I say slowly. "To remind you that it's not a big life-and-death struggle. He made you for Marie, his niece. To be played with. To be loved."

The Nutcracker smiles—for real, for a moment. I see real teeth, a real face, under that endless grin. Then he transforms all the way, and he's a man. A normal, beautiful man in a ragged costume. His smile is still huge, but in a good way. Beaming. "Thank you, Clara."

He steps forward and repeats what he said at the beginning, in that singsong:

> *"One battle ended,*
> *Two links forged,*
> *Those who are lost shall be found."*

He lifts one hand, in blessing or goodbye. "Well done."

They vanish, all of them, except me and Noah. Even the Nutcracker. Just like that, one moment to the next. Their swords are gone too, and any evidence that they were here. The workshop is empty, still, the only movement the flickering of the candles.

"Do you think they went somewhere else?" I ask Noah. "To the Kingdom of Sweets, home, to be happy? Or did they just disappear into thin air?" I imagine Grandpa Reynolds, locked in his own world, and swallow hard. "I don't want them to just disappear."

Noah shrugs. "I don't know. But . . . let's say they didn't. It's a story, after all. We're the only ones here. We can choose how it ends." He smiles big. "You saved them, and they got to go home. In peace."

In peace. I wonder suddenly what the Nutcracker's puzzle means, if I'm supposed to understand now. The battle is ended—that I know. That we accomplished.

"We did it," I say, the words a drop in the quiet.

"We did it," Noah echoes. "And now we can go home."

"How did you get here?" I ask. "Where *are* you, really?"

"The bugle," he says. He holds it up, still in his hand, and smiles again. "In the toy museum, right by my house. I used to go there all the time and look at everything for hours. I recognized it." He shrugs. "I took it from the display and sneaked into a closet in the storage room, and I played it, just to see. It worked."

I laugh. "Yeah, it worked. Though you could've told me first."

He grimaces. "Probably would've been a good idea. Anyway, I can get home from there, easy. If we can get back. How do we get back if we're both here and there's nothing to pull us out?"

I look around the workshop one more time, at all the tables and toys, at the big grandfather clock in the corner. "I've got a backup, just in case. But I think the magic's broken, with all of them gone. I think we can probably go home whenever we want to now. Try. You go first."

He grins at me once more, does a little bow, and disappears.

I take a deep breath and close my eyes.

Then I open them into the darkness of the balcony stairs.

# 29

**The Nutcracker isn't warm** anymore, doesn't tingle or anything. He feels like he should, like a toy. I have to put him back, then call home. I set him in his box, but I don't close it yet. I pull back the curtain of my hiding place, so tired.

I nearly stumble across Kaitlyn, sitting right next to the door, her knees pulled to her chest. She looks up and smiles. "Hey."

"You're here!" I slide down next to her. The wall feels strong against my back, holding me up. "How did you get in?"

"You think you're the only one who can be sneaky? I got here as fast as I could after you called, and sneaked in between techs. I look like a dancer, remember? And I know

220

the place. I was ready to get you out if I had to. Just like you said on the phone." She pokes me in the side, jerks her chin at the Nutcracker. "How'd it go? Did you find Noah?"

"He's fine. Should be back now, and he can go home. We . . . finished it."

She raises her eyebrows at me.

"I'll explain later, I promise. It's too much now. But the Nutcracker is safe. All of them are safe."

She nods. She reaches out and touches the Nutcracker's painted cheek with one finger. "Troublemaker."

"I didn't expect you to come. I just wanted to tell you what was happening, as backup in case I didn't show up at home tonight. So someone knew where I was. I didn't think you'd *come*."

"I know." Again, the Kaitlyn smile, the one I missed so much. "But I wanted to be part of it. Even if it's only at the end."

I want to hug her too, like I did Noah, but it'd be awkward, sitting down with the Nutcracker on my lap. I squeeze her hand instead, and she squeezes back.

"Best friends," I say.

She grins. "Best friends. Always."

Even if we do different things, I think we'll stick together.

*Two links forged.* I wonder if that's what it meant. Me and Kaitlyn, back together again. And me and Noah brought together. It makes sense. But what was lost? Was that our friendship too?

Slowly I get to my feet, move to the prop table, and set the box where it should be, all the way back against the wall. I touch the Nutcracker's face too. I don't say anything, though. It's already been said. I loved him, and I think that was enough. I close the lid.

"I guess I'd better call my mom to pick me up," I say. "Face the music."

"Are you kidding?" Kaitlyn asks. "It's almost ten-thirty. Why do you think I brought my bike?"

**The wind is cold** against my face as I sit in front of Kaitlyn on her handlebars. I don't care. I feel like my happiness in this one moment could warm everything. Noah's safe, the Nutcracker's back where he should be—home, wherever that is—and Kaitlyn and I are friends again. Noah and I are friends. We did it. Now I just have to go home, tell one more lie, and I'm done. I can still be Clara, and it will mean so much more.

But when we pull up in front of my house, the car and the truck are gone. The lights are on inside, but the driveway is empty.

They must be out looking for me. That's bad. With all the lies, the hiding, they probably will take away Clara. That will be the price I pay for saving the Nutcracker and Noah: not getting to be Clara after all.

It'll kill me. But it'll be worth it.

"Want me to come in with you?" Kaitlyn asks softly.

I jump off the handlebars. "No. You'd better stay out of it as much as you can." I frown at her. "How did you explain where you were, out so late?"

She laughs. "My mom thinks you're crazy, but she wants us to be friends again. She said I'm a mess without you. I said you needed me, and I'd be back soon. I texted her from the theater that I was okay. And again when we were leaving." She pushes off, heading home. "See you tomorrow. You and Noah are going to tell me the whole story, promise?"

"Promise," I say. "Thanks, Kait." I watch her until she

gets to the end of the block. Then I go inside, expecting fireworks. Though I don't know who's here, if Mom and Dad are both gone. . . .

"Hey," says the babysitter, Lisa. She's sitting on the sofa doing homework, playing music low from her phone. She lives three doors down and has been our babysitter since she was in middle school; she's a senior in high school now. "Your mom said you'd be late, but I didn't think *this* late. They work you hard, huh?"

I drop next to her on the sofa. I'm not in trouble? At all? "What's going on? You weren't supposed to be here, were you?"

"Emergency call from your mom. The hospital called about your grandpa, and she and your dad had to take off."

All the warmth, that happiness, drains out of my body. No. Not now. I grip the edge of the sofa as hard as I can. I feel the prick of the staples against my fingers. "Is he going to . . . die?"

Lisa closes the book and leans forward, her hair swinging around her face. "No, munchkin. He woke up. It'll be a while—he's got to recover. He can't talk yet. But they think he's going to be okay."

I can't speak. I only nod, then cry, tears dripping down my face. Then laugh and cry at the same time while Lisa hugs me.

"He's going to be okay," I repeat into her shoulder.

The last piece of me, the piece that was sad about Grandpa through everything, clicks into place.

He's going to be okay. Different, but okay. It all is.

*Those who are lost shall be found.*

I don't think it means a relationship. I think it means *Grandpa*. I don't know if it was a promise—if I helped, if we succeeded—or a prophecy. But it's all come true. The battle is ended. Two friendships are solid now. And Grandpa is found.

# 30

**The last week of rehearsal** is a blur. Rehearsals every day, for every scene, until I actually dance them in my sleep, in my dreams. I don't even have school from here on—once we get into the intensive rehearsals, we get excused from school until the end of the run. We have to do all our homework, of course, on breaks and whenever we're not needed onstage.

I miss Kaitlyn and Noah . . . when I have time to miss anything. Mostly it's rehearse, rehearse, rehearse, eat, sleep, rehearse. But I'll see both Kaitlyn and Noah tonight, after the show.

My opening night.

I stand on the stage in my Clara costume, my hair

in stiff, perfect ringlets, heavy on my shoulders. The clothes aren't the same, of course, and the set is a pale shadow of the grand ballroom in the Nutcracker's world, but it is a strange echo. As close as I'll get to being there again.

The audience whispers and rustles on the other side of the curtain. My whole family is in the theater tonight to see me: even Joey and Pippa and Will, dressed up in fancy clothes. Pip is wearing the same green velvet dress I wore the first time I came with Grandpa. She loves it, twirling around and around while it swirls. Joey's wearing a dress too. She gave me a little Nutcracker, my very own, before the performance today. Mom said she bought it with her own money.

Noah's there too with his family—his mom and dad on either side of him. I'm not sure what he told them about why he was missing, but they just look happy to have him back.

And Kaitlyn and her mom are there, too. They're sitting with Noah and his family. We're all friends now. We're the only ones who know the secret.

Well, and one other person. Grandpa Reynolds can't be here—he can't leave the hospital yet—but Mrs. Cavanaugh said we could get him a copy of the video performance of tonight. They're taping tonight, instead of first cast at dress rehearsal, just for me. I know he'll love it. I know he'll be so proud that I did it after all.

"Seven minutes!" the stage manager calls behind me, and I close my eyes. It's now. Magic time.

"Georgie!" There's a tug on my hand. It's Justin, in his bright blue suit, with his slicked-down yellow hair. "C'mon," he says, excited. "Let's peek at the audience!"

I don't even consider it. I've broken enough rules already. I squeeze his hand, let go. "We have a show to do. Let's get in our places, and we can listen to the audience from there. See if we can hear them."

He shrugs. "Okay." He runs off to our place, feet thumping so loud the audience can probably hear it. The stage manager frowns, but I don't care. I feel like I could float right now, the contentment so strong it could carry me right up into the rigging without even needing a balloon.

"It's here, Nutcracker," I whisper. "My first performance. Are you ready?"

"Are *you* ready?" Mrs. Cavanaugh says, behind me.

I look up over my shoulder and smile, a little nervous. Her face is stern, like always. "I think so," I say.

She nods thoughtfully, then rests one hand on my shoulder. We stand there for a moment looking out on the stage together, listening to the murmur of the audience.

"It's magical to dance with him, isn't it?" she says, low.

I go very still, my breath loud in my ears. She *knows*.

I knew it.

"It is," I whisper.

"I believe he's ready now. And that you are too. Well done, Georgie." She pats my shoulder, brisk. "Go on, then. Make me proud."

I walk carefully across the stage to my place. I look back once, but she's gone, vanished into the wings.

The orchestra starts the overture, and the lights go dark. Justin and I wait in the wings together, listening. It's so beautiful I want to cry. And throw up a little. But I rock on my feet in my new ballet slippers and wait, wait, until the curtain opens and the stage lights come on. It's our music.

I dance out onto the stage as Clara.

**It's amazing, all of it.** Every moment.

But there's one part I didn't expect, and it's my very favorite.

It happens in the tree-growing scene. Even after all the rehearsals it's eerie going onstage by myself, in the near dark, with my little stage candle. It's almost but not quite as scary as the real thing. I imagine I can smell the candles and the tree as I watch the massive room grow around me, the sets pulling up to reveal furniture higher than my head. I hug the Nutcracker, my Nutcracker, all alone as the music flows around me, then jump as the clock chimes. I hear the mice-men scurrying behind me, though I'm not supposed to see them yet.

*"Watch out, Clara!"*

It comes from the audience, a high, clear voice, obviously a little girl. A mouse-man behind me laughs; it's so unexpected and loud. But my eyes fill instantly.

That girl—whoever she is—is so wrapped up in the show, believes it so hard, that she's actually worrying about me. *Me.* I've become Clara to her, as real as a friend.

We did that, me and all the other dancers working so

hard, making it happen. And maybe someday that little girl will want to be a dancer too. Like I did when I was five and I watched Clara beat the Mouse King. Maybe she *will* be a dancer.

The tree grows and I hold my candle up to it, the full orchestra playing behind me.

The Nutcracker may be gone to his home, and I may be only in this world now. But this is magic.

Real, true magic, everywhere.

# Acknowledgments

This book began with a tweet.

I tweeted in 2012 that I really should write that *Nutcracker* middle-grade book I'd been pondering for so long . . . and a good friend replied that I should write it NOW. It was my first attempt at a middle-grade title, but I forged ahead with that story, and the first draft of this book was born. Thanks, Molly O'Neill. Good call.

It's been a long and winding road since then, but I am so thrilled that *Nutcracked* landed at Random House with my wonderful editors, Jenna Lettice and Michelle Nagler, who have been as supportive, inspiring, and smart as any author could hope for. Huge thanks also to Caroline Abbey for stepping in and guiding me through one last edit. Thank you to my Random House team, including copyeditors Barbara Bakowski and Alison Kolani, production supervisor Nathan Kinney, and designer Elizabeth Tardiff, and to cover illustrator Stevie Lewis. I love how you brought Georgie to life!

Thank you always to my superagent, Kate Schafer

Testerman, who is my champion and confidant in all things publishing.

I would never succeed without the support and business sense of my husband, Michael, and the boundless optimism of my daughter, Sophie. Thank you always.

Thank you to the wonderful community of YA and middle-grade authors, who support each other at every turn. I am so happy to call many of you friends and colleagues.

*Nutcracked*, which is partly about ballet and goals, is dedicated to my mom, who made sure I could be Clara if I wanted to be and who took me to classes and auditions and rehearsals for years. She later transferred that encouragement to my writing and is still my biggest fan. Thank you, Mom. You'll recognize a lot in these pages. And thanks to Doc, who's always been there when I needed him.

This book is also dedicated to Mrs. Crockett, who was the artistic director of the Sacramento Ballet when I danced there. She taught me real discipline, fitted my first pointe shoes, and chose me to be one of her Claras, and I will forever be grateful. It truly was magic.

# About the Author

**Susan Adrian** is a fourth-generation Californian who now lives in the beautiful Big Sky country of Montana. She began ballet late—at age eight—but got to fulfill her dream of playing Clara in *The Nutcracker* when she was thirteen, with the Sacramento Ballet. Later she got a degree in English from the University of California, Davis. These days she's settled in as a writer, scientific editor, and mom. When she's not with her family, she keeps busy researching crazy stuff, traveling, and writing more books. She still sees *The Nutcracker* every year she can, and tries really hard not to act out all the parts.